CAMP
OFF-THE-WALL

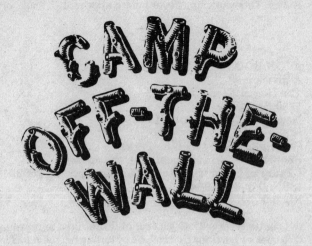

CAMP OFF-THE-WALL

CAM PARKER

AN AVON CAMELOT BOOK

CAMP OFF-THE-WALL is an original publication of Avon Books. This work has never before appeared in book form.

AVON BOOKS
A division of
The Hearst Corporation
1790 Broadway
New York, New York 10019

Copyright © 1987 by Cam Parker
Published by arrangement with the author
Library of Congress Catalog Card Number: 86-25921
ISBN: 0-380-75196-8
RL: 6.0

Library of Congress Cataloging in Publication Data:

Parker, Cam.
  Camp off-the-wall.

  "An Avon Camelot book"
  Summary: Seventh-grader Tiffin and fourth-grader Wil's parents separate before sending the children off to summer camps—then spend the summer on the doorsteps of the camps, scrapping and working out their relationship.
  [1. Marriage—Fiction. 2. Camps—Fiction] I. Title.
PZ7.P2219Cam   1987   [Fic]   86-25921

First Camelot Printing: April 1987

CAMELOT TRADEMARK REG. U.S. PAT. OFF. AND IN OTHER COUNTRIES, MARCA REGISTRADA, HECHO EN U.S.A.

Printed in the U.S.A.

OPM   10   9   8   7   6   5   4   3   2   1

To Scott, Xenia, and
All the Horses at Claremont

Chapter One

My name is Tiffin. It's not short for Tiffany, it's just plain Tiffin. Tiffin Roswell. My parents named me after a town in Ohio where they first met. They were in college at the time. My brother, who's three years younger than I am, is named Wilmington, after the town in Delaware my mother and father eloped to after Mama finished law school. I'm just grateful they didn't stumble across each other in Puyallup, Washington, or Muskogee, Oklahoma. Going through life as a Tiffin is hard enough, believe me.

Sometimes it seems that nothing makes going through life easy, and this year, the going got just a little more rugged. First I got upper and lower braces on my teeth, giving me a smile like a brand-new bicycle chain. Then I found out that we were all in for a drastic change of plans. This was the year we were all supposed to go on an ocean cruise: the Bahamas, Bermuda, or Staten Island even. It was supposed to be a second honeymoon for my parents and a broadening experience for my brother Wil and me.

But then, on the day after Mother's Day no less, my parents separated. They said they were doing it for the good of the children—and it would be good for the children to go to camp.

What had happened? Wil and I used to wonder. What had happened between these two people who used to positively embarrass us with their public displays of affection towards each other? It seemed to have started when Mama didn't like the birthday present my father bought her. It was an entire half of a hickory-smoked salmon that Daddy ordered from a mail-order catalogue.

Wil and I thought it was wonderful, especially with a little lemon and a touch of freshly ground pepper. I was developing my taste buds as a gourmet and had never tasted anything so delicious. But Mama got very upset. I think she was expecting something a little more personal. As it was, she'd just gotten over the steam iron he'd given her for Valentine's Day.

I assumed she'd get over this as well, and we did seriously talk about our planned cruise one night during the week between Mama's birthday and Mother's Day. My parents had wine with dinner, and then we all watched a shipboard love story on the small color set in their room. It was about an older couple who recapture romance on the ship without falling overboard. It seemed to inspire my father, and somehow we all got excited about that cruise. Daddy walked around spouting "second honeymoon" for days. Mama even agreed to pay half the fare, and it got positively lovey-dovey around the house right up to Mother's Day. That's when Dad got her this terrific microwave oven that could sit on the kitchen counter and not take up much space at all.

That morning he unwrapped it carefully and carried it into their room on tiptoe. We followed and woke up Mama by shouting "Surprise!" She looked at her present and turned absolutely purple.

She said, "This is the last straw." Then she said she didn't want to be in the same room with my father, and then she stopped talking altogether. I believe she wanted flowers.

Even so, I couldn't see why she got so upset over presents. I never get any presents I really want. Not for my birthday or for any other holiday for that matter. But heaven forbid that I should get upset, even a little upset. Then I get the speech about how I should be thankful for what I got, and how, if I kept up such ungrateful complaining, next year I wouldn't get anything, and see how I'd like that.

After Mama reacted to her birthday gift that way, Wil and I thought that perhaps it was an allergic reaction to freshly ground pepper, or lemon, or smoked food. Then, after the Mother's Day incident, we thought that perhaps she was allergic to Daddy. The next morning they announced that Wil and I were going to camp that summer—and they were going their separate ways on a trial basis!

Mama, being a lawyer, offered to explain the legal aspects of the situation, and Daddy, being a psychologist, offered to explain the psychological aspects of the situation. Wil and I both groaned.

Then they said that we would love going to camp this year.

"You'll love going to camp this year," Daddy said.

"You'll love going to camp this year," Mama said. "And you can go to whatever kind of camp you like."

"I'll hate going to camp," I said. "Especially under these conditions." But by that time, nobody except Wil was listening.

Even I, who was saying those words—and hearing and listening besides—was shocked at what I was saying. I wanted to go to camp. Horse camp. A real horse camp, where there'd be a horse for me to ride and groom and say good morning and good night to. Someplace where they'd never heard of basket weaving or poster paints. Strictly horses, and maybe a swimming pool.

I'd dreamed of it. But, first of all, my parents had always been too cheap to send me, especially my father. He admits it. He's proud of it. He says that as a psychologist, it's a sign of his good mental health to admit his cheapness. My mother says that legally she agrees with him, but morally it's disgraceful for any one person to be so stingy. He's not Scrooge exactly, and they give me an allowance. Between that and the Saturday afternoons I spend at the stables surrounded by saddles and bridles—cleaning tack in exchange for riding—I get to take a lesson once a month on my favorite horse, Tartan.

I love horses. I always have. There's something fine and noble about them, and no horse ever told me to believe in the tooth fairy or Santa Claus. I told my parents that once, and they said they'd have to think about it. They may still be thinking about it. We certainly never talked about it again. As for Wil, he'd always wanted to go to soccer camp, but they were too cheap to send him, too. When we found out how much that cruise was going to cost them, Wil and I almost fainted. When it came to second honeymoons, price was no problem. But that's parents for you; that's why they have children's menus in restaurants. Besides,

4

for a few days between presents, Wil and I thought we'd saved their marriage and our household by agreeing to go on that cruise, and that I could go back to thinking about horses full-time and he could kick his soccer ball in peace.

Instead, here was Mama talking about trial separations, and here was Daddy talking about subletting one of his patients' apartments. It sounded very unhealthy to me.

"We're doing this for you and your brother," they both said at the same time. They explained reasonably, and together again, how Wil and I would be better off without them. Without them together, that is. "It's for the good of the children," they said simultaneously, and looked at each other, and nodded in agreement. For people breaking up, they certainly were being agreeable.

I told them that I, along with my brother Wil and everybody else I'd ever heard of or knew, was under the impression that parents stayed married for the good of the children.

"They don't break up after Mother's Day and send the kids to camp for the good of the children," I said as firmly as I could under the circumstances. Even my brother Wil, in one of the last times anybody saw him outside his room willingly that spring, shouted that he was going to hate camp, too. I agreed.

My parents were having none of it. "There are problems you don't understand," Mama said. "You're much too young yet." That's the same thing she'd said the time I asked her about sex. She blushed and said it was not the time to discuss it—we were sitting on the crosstown bus.

Where my parents' problems were concerned, it wasn't the ones I didn't understand that was the problem. The problem was the problems I didn't even know about! I always thought we had a relatively happy home life going for us. We never really heard them arguing about anything much. Mostly, in times of stress, they stopped talking to each other altogether. I thought it was all very civilized. At least it was quiet. I have a friend whose parents don't seem to get along, and her house sounds like a bowling alley.

The closest my parents came to a disagreement in front of Wil and me, that I remembered anyway, was the one about where we should live. Daddy said the city was full of fumes and short tempers. He wanted to live in the country, or at least the suburbs. Mama said that the city was pulsing with life and opportunity, and her office was within walking distance of our apartment. Even that difference of opinion didn't seem to be earthshaking, let alone home-wrecking. That conversation seemed to come up only when Daddy watched a nature program on television. My mother would usually say that he'd get over it, and he usually did. It just goes to show that you never can tell.

Wil seemed to take the news of the impending breakup fairly well. His main concern was whether or not he got to keep his room.

"My poor darling," Mama said and swept across the living room. She gathered Wil into her arms and attempted to lift him, but he's getting a little too big for that kind of thing. Instead, she crushed him to her side and mashed his nose against her arm. "Your room will always be there for you," she said nobly. "And so will your mother." She looked at Daddy accusingly and hugged Wil even closer. By this time he was having difficulty breathing, and the one eye I was able to see peering under my mother's elbow began to turn

6

glassy. He gulped for precious oxygen, but the sound he made while swallowing air sounded, to my mother at least, like a sob.

"My poor darling," she repeated emotionally and scowled even more fiercely at Dad. Then she saw me standing there across the room and decided to include me in her embrace as well. She hugged Wil even tighter, dragged him to me, and flung her free arm around my waist. The three of us stood clinging together like a bunch of grapes, and Daddy kind of shuffled his feet and looked guilty.

"Tiffin," my mother assured me, "your room, and I, will always be there for you, too."

I said that as long as that was the case, and as long as our rooms would always be there, would she mind if we used them over the summer instead of going to camp. Then maybe we could all go on the new-beginnings second-honeymoon, and we could all stay together.

"After all," I reminded them, "you two were supposed to take us on a cruise this summer." My mother let go of us, and the four of us sat down to have a Family Discussion—that's generally always bad news. First they said that perhaps Mama could take us on a cruise. Then they said that perhaps Daddy could take us on a cruise. Then they said that nobody was going to take us on a cruise.

"You mean," said Wil, looking excited about the prospect for the first time, "that we can go by ourselves?"

I think that hurt their feelings or something, because they got a little quiet for a minute or two and repeated that we were going to camp and they were going their separate ways. The Family Discussion had ended. Wil got up from his seat looking sad, and

Mama grabbed him again. I rose and headed for the kitchen, but she snared me just behind the sofa. Wil managed to get his nose free enough to snort that he had to go to the bathroom. Mama quickly released him. I said that I had to go to the bathroom too, and she let go of me as well.

When Wil came out of the bathroom, he looked at us all and then went to his room to tell his belongings that they didn't have to move. I took his place in the bathroom until it got dark out and Mama knocked on the door.

In the weeks that followed Daddy's sudden departure from our daily lives, his chair, and the apartment, we experimented with explanations for their odd behavior. Since we saw Daddy only Wednesday nights and weekends, and since Mama was the one who got so angry, we concentrated on her. We microwaved everything in sight. We ground fresh pepper into her hamburgers and squeezed lemon onto her salads, but she never once got upset. She told us we were wonderful children and sighed a lot.

Maybe it had been the fish, we thought. But as it turned out, she didn't seem to be allergic to that after all. In fact, she seemed to like it. She'd frozen what we couldn't eat at the time—and who could eat at that time, anyway—and when she had what she called her emancipation party several weeks after the big breakup, she ate it just fine, lemon, pepper, and all.

Daddy, in his visits over the following weeks, came loaded with psychological explanations about why sending us to camp was just what we needed in our situation. He said it would give us a chance to meet other kids whose parents were separated, other kids in the same boat. Wil said he already knew lots of other kids whose parents were separated. He said the boat was already full; it seemed to him that almost everybody in his fourth-grade class was in it.

That seemed to make Daddy feel less guilty. He sighed—he'd been doing that a lot lately—and then he sat heavily in what used to be called Daddy's chair. We didn't call it that anymore. Whenever we did, my mother got a headache and we'd have to fix our own dinner. Our poodle, Fluff, who Mama brought home as a present the week after Daddy left, slept in the chair all day long. Mama began calling it the dog's chair. She seemed to get a lot of satisfaction out of doing that; it cheered her up quite a bit.

The only reason Fluff wasn't asleep in the chair at the time of my father's visit was that we had to keep her in the bedroom with the door closed whenever Daddy came by. She just loved to nip at his feet right where his shoes and ankles met. She was awfully good at it, too. The first time they were introduced, Daddy had to do a tap dance to escape. He went out the door like a nervous flamenco dancer.

After that, Mama told us to exile Fluff while Daddy was there. She said she wasn't worried about Daddy, but she didn't want the dog to get overexcited; it was no good for her fur, it made her shed. Then too, she didn't want Fluff getting sick if she ever managed to take a real bite out of Dad's foot.

"You'll love camp," Daddy said to us, just a little feebly. He sighed again and got up and went to the window. He looked down into the street to check on his double-parked car. Seeing that it was still safe, he went back to his chair, but before he sat down, he noticed all the fur on it. He quickly began brushing dog hairs from the seat of his pants as he looked at us both with his oh-cruel-world expression.

"I thought poodles weren't supposed to shed," he

said as he did every time he came to visit and sat in what used to be his chair. When he finished doing that, he paced around the living room and told me that the whole world loved going to camp, just to see if either of us was convinced. Then he sighed contentedly, as if something had been settled in somebody's mind other than his.

Suddenly the bell on the intercom rang urgently, three times. It was the doorman signaling an alert. Daddy rushed to the window and looked down to the street below to see if his illegally double-parked car was being towed away.

Finding a place to park even for a few minutes is a big worry in the city, especially since it costs about a hundred dollars to get a car out of the clutches of the traffic department once they get their hands on it.

First, Daddy gasped. Then, Daddy shouted, "A tow truck!" Then Daddy fell over what used to be his chair in his hurry to get to the elevator and rush to the rescue of his besieged automobile.

He'd almost reached the door when Fluff somehow worked her way out of the bedroom. She spotted his feet leaving the apartment and chased him down the hall. In a way she was doing him a favor, because he reached the elevator in record time. Luckily for him, he got in a split second before Fluff could, and the doors closed gently in her barking face. Unluckily for him, poodles are pretty smart dogs, and Fluff was no exception. She sized up the situation and raced down the stairs.

Mama heard the commotion and came into the living room from the kitchen, where she'd been busy inspecting the crockery while Daddy was visiting. I'm not sure what she was looking for there among the dishes, but it certainly held her attention when my father was in the vicinity.

When they first began what they refer to as "the arrangement," she'd just go out of the apartment when there was no Family Discussion scheduled and the doorman called up on the intercom to say that Dad was on his way. She even took up jogging for a while and would sprint out the door as Daddy came in. She did that on all but cool or rainy days, but after a few weeks she got tired of running around the block, so she began to retreat to the kitchen instead to rattle the pots and pans. It always seemed such a wonder to me that two people who'd been married, and, if you'll excuse the expression, intimate for so many years just suddenly couldn't spend six minutes in the same room together. I asked her why she was treating Daddy this way, and she said she'd tell me at another time.

Mama looked around the room, and seeing just us, asked, "Where did *he* go?" forgetting all the times in the long-ago past that she'd yelled at us for referring to Daddy as *he* instead of Daddy. But that was before the separation. Now *he* was in, while Daddy was out.

Mama didn't wait for an answer. She walked to the window herself and looked down as the tow truck slowly raised our car's front end into towing position. The special burglar alarm we'd installed so no one would steal the car—that's another big worry when you live in the city—went off as the car went up. The horn started to honk, the siren started to howl, the lights started to blink on and off, and just then Daddy came racing out of the building with Fluff racing after him.

"Wait! Wait!" he shouted as he ran and hopped and tried to avoid sticking his ankle into Fluff's teeth.

"Wait!" he called to the tow truck operator and skipped across the sidewalk into the street. "Wait!"

But the tow truck operator did not wait. He saw Daddy running, shouting, jumping, and being followed closely by a snapping dog. Poor man. I suppose he thought he had a crazed car owner and an attack poodle coming after him. He jumped into the front seat of his truck and drove off as fast as he could.

Poor Daddy went racing down the street after him, chasing his honking, screeching, blinking car while Fluff chased him.

"Wait!" he shouted. "Wait!"

First Mama just smiled. Then she chuckled until it turned into a big loud laugh, and finally I thought she was going to roll around on the floor in glee. For a second it occurred to me that she might be having some kind of a fit. I have to admit it was nice to see her so happy. "I hope they keep it this time," she shouted through the window glass. Then she sighed a deep, satisfied sigh—she'd been doing that a lot lately, too. The tow truck and Daddy's car reached the corner with my father in hot pursuit and gaining on his property.

"Faster," Mama called to the tow truck. "You can drive faster than that!" Then, almost as it could hear her ten stories down and a half block away, the truck dragging its precious cargo picked up speed and turned the corner on two wheels, leaving Daddy panting for air and dancing desperately across the sidewalk with Fluff.

Chapter Two

It was shortly after that incident that camp brochures began to arrive mysteriously in the mail. First one or two a week, then one or two a day.

"They probably got our names from a mailing list someplace. Maybe from one of our magazine subscriptions," I said in my most hopeful but unconvinced tone of voice. We were still at the hoping-they'd-get-together phase. I looked to my parents to confirm this optimistic viewpoint, but Mama busied herself with some of the work she brings home from the office. Daddy, on the other hand, just looked at his watch—something he always does when he has more to say, but won't.

Then one day Wil and I received the brochure that was to decide our fate. It was a full-color videotape sent for blatantly and behind my back. It came complete with inspiring narration and a sound track from *The Sound of Music*. *See* the inmates to play. *See* the

Sunday barbecue with everyone looking sick. *See* the staff sharpening their teeth. Camp Chucalucup was beckoning, and my parents were heeding the call. Part of me was thrilled, but I finally understood what the expression *mixed emotions* meant. It all seemed very symbolic in a way, my parents leaving each other, us leaving them.

"Horses!" Mama said happily to me the night she saw the video. "You love horses; you'll be able to ride horses."

"I don't have to go to Chucalucup to ride horses," I said in vain. "I can love them at a distance for a while. From the deck of a cruise ship for instance, on a full family-plan fare."

"Horses," Daddy said happily the night he saw the video. "You both love horses."

"I hate horses," Wil declared. "They make me itch. They make me sneeze. They make me want to throw up." He thought that sounded so good that he repeated it for my mother the following day.

"I thought you'd say that," Mama said lightly. And she gave Wil the good news. It seemed that Daddy had discovered quite some time back—even before she sent for the video—that there was a horseless boys' camp just across the lake from Camp Chucalucup. They'd discussed it. It seems my parents got along fine over the phone. "And guess what one of their specialties is?" Mama asked Wil, full of good cheer.

"Teaching how to cope with single parents?" Wil asked brightly. Mama chuckled.

"No darling, soccer, darling, soccer." That wrapped us both neatly up in one tight bow. She rewound the tape and we all watched it again.

"Isn't that lovely?" Mama asked every time the music got low enough to be heard over. Whenever

Daddy saw it, he'd say the same thing. Between the two of them, Wil and I had to watch that video five times. Throughout it all, we looked at each other much in the same way we did the night we found out that the family was breaking up for our sake.

This was beginning to look like one of those foregone conclusions I'd heard so much about. An arrangement where everything's been arranged in advance. It starts with "We're here to talk some things over," and it goes right from there to "Case closed." This time around, we were almost definitely going to camp for our sake.

This was tentatively decided at one of our Family Discussion Forums. These were held, in case of emergencies and against Mama's will, during Daddy's midweek visits, on Wednesdays. We'd always had them on that day before they separated, so that stayed the same when we became two single-parent families. My parents used the occasion of their both being there to team up on us. Usually, we saw them separately, and believe me, they were a lot easier to handle that way. When they got together, that was another scoreboard. Parents 2, children 0.

Wil and I decided to apply the logic we'd so often heard from our parents concerning our moods and wants. "They'll get over it," they'd say. Now we started to say it, sometimes twice a day. "They'll get over it."

We contented ourselves thinking that, and life, such as it had become, went on in our household. Mama spent a good deal of time reminding us that she didn't want to be reminded of Daddy, and Daddy kept reminding us to remind him to check on his car. We kept watch on Wednesday nights, when the competition for a parking space could get fierce. It seemed that every father in the neighborhood showed up on Wednesday nights to see his kids—and all of them showed up by car. People in the neighborhood can always tell it's Wednesday just by the sight of the fathers running in and out of the buildings to protect their cars.

It was just one such Wednesday night that sealed our fates for good, as far as the summer was concerned. Daddy was coming by to pick us up for dinner. We usually went to a restaurant, and a different one each time. Then the three of us sat there and pretended to enjoy dinner under those circumstances. Daddy used to take us to his apartment to eat when he first moved into it. By this time though, the dishes had eaten his sink, and the only usable utensils in the place were his morning-coffee cup and a gleaming teaspoon. These Daddy kept clean by washing them in the bathroom sink before and after each use. I couldn't understand why he washed them both before and after, but Wil said Dad was overcompensating for not having washed the rest of the plates and cutlery. What made things worse was that my father had two sets of dishes and flatware; he'd gotten them all from a neighborhood bank where he opened a new account after he found the apartment. Now all of it, starting with sixteen pieces of everything, had overflowed the basin and spread out onto the counter. He said what he needed was another new account somewhere.

We did try to wash all of them once, the three of us, but we ran out of dishwashing soap before we reached the second layer. That night was the first night Daddy ever said anything about missing Mama. We were standing there trying to wring the last drop of detergent from its plastic bottle, and Daddy said, "Your mother would know how to handle this." Then he sighed.

Wil and I looked upon that utterance with leaping hopes. He did miss Mama, even if only for her dishwashing capabilities. That was better than not being missed at all, we decided. After the last of the pots and pans joined the pile, Daddy stopped cooking his overdone chicken and underdone potatoes, and our restaurant tour began.

There were some benefits to eating out alone with my father. He began to let us order drinks like Shirley Temples, and piña coladas without the rum. That last one is Wil's favorite drink, but in days gone by, we weren't allowed to order them except on special occasions, like when our grandparents took us out, or when Mama was entertaining a special client, or when Daddy wanted to show one of his patients the benefits of family life. On those special occasions, my parents didn't like to shout *No* at us in public. They saved all their *No*'s for when we got home.

This particular Wednesday evening had started on a note of high hope. Just before my father got there, I looked out the window and saw a real live legal parking space right in front of our house. Wil, Fluff, and I rushed downstairs to guard it from everybody else's visiting father. "It's taken, it's taken," we shouted at every driver who drove up hopefully. Some of them wanted to park anyway, but we wouldn't move out of the street, and Fluff did her share by barking continuously. When our father drove up, he was thrilled to see the space and us waiting, but he wouldn't get out of the car until after we got Fluff out of the way. We put her in the back seat as Daddy quickly exited the front.

In celebration of not having to guard the car, Daddy decided that we should walk to a neighborhood Chinese restaurant we all used to go to when our parents lived together. Wil and I decided that was a good sign. Maybe he was getting nostalgic for the old days; maybe he'd come courting. I was happy to be going there, because we hadn't in a long time. The people are very nice, and what we really liked about it was that they had booths.

The couple who owns the restaurant seemed very happy to see us, and dinner went very nicely—at first.

We'd just finished a dessert of green mint-tea ice cream and almond cookies. Green mint-tea is not my favorite ice cream flavor, but it's all they serve, and it sounds healthy. That night, Wil ordered his favorite drink, and the bartender, who knows us by now, poured the mixture of coconut juice and pineapple into one glass for Wil and topped it with a huge fresh strawberry and a whole Maraschino cherry on a stem. Then he put a paper umbrella into the drink. After he finished admiring his creation, he took the alcohol part of the drink, in this case rum, and poured it into a glass of cracked ice for Daddy.

Daddy really doesn't like rum over ice, or rum anyway at all. However, since he started letting Wil order as if it were a special occasion, he decided to cultivate a taste for it. Besides, he says he's much too cheap to pay for it and let it go to waste, so he drinks part of it slowly and with great sacrifice.

That early June evening was the night that Daddy got the news. Wil had just finished his second piña colada and looked up at Daddy. Then he asked very casually, "Can I ask you a question, Dad?"

"Of course you can, son," Dad said and looked attentive. He sat up in his seat, reached into the inside pocket of his suit jacket, and took out his conversation glasses. Then he put them on and peered expectantly at Wil. "Wil," he said sincerely, "there is no question that you cannot ask your father. None, ever. That's one of the things I'm here for. To answer your questions, to help you grow. You too, Tiffin," he added, looking very concerned and ready to help. "What is it you want to know, Wil?" he inquired gently.

"What I want to know, Dad, is do I have to call Mama's next husband Daddy, too?"

Chapter Three

Our father decided to treat the question as a request for general information. He said that he was our daddy, he always had been our daddy, and furthermore would always be our daddy—our number-one, first-and-last daddy. That's his number-one, top-priority speech. We've heard it so many times that the three of us can recite it in unison.

He finished assuring us until he felt assured, and then there was quiet. The check came, and instead of signing it and us getting up and leaving, Daddy asked me if I wanted a Shirley Temple. Then he offered Wil another piña colada. It was clear that he didn't want to end the conversation until he found out whether Wil was talking specifics here.

Dad wanted to know if this was the usual question of concern from a child from an almost-broken home, or was there currently some sign of a new daddy on the horizon?

"Is there anything you'd like to discuss with me?" he asked in a supercalm voice full of *I won't yell, you can tell me anything.*

We waited a minute in silence. Then he said, "You know I won't yell; you can tell me anything."

All three of us began to fidget at the same time. Daddy bent the little plastic bar straws in half, and Wil made rings on the table with the wet bottom of his piña colada glass. I practiced standing my chopsticks on end.

We continued to sit in our comfortable restaurant booth while we waited for Wil to tell Daddy the "anything" he seemed prepared to hear. But no sound came out of Wil. The waiter who'd brought our check came back to the table three times, and I couldn't drink any more water. Finally Daddy paid it, but we still just sat there. Daddy began to bend the already-mangled bar straws in half again, and my chopsticks continued their refusal to stand up.

Wil finally began to talk, but he began to talk about his dismal efforts at fourth-grade math. "My teacher hates me," he said. "And you're supposed to have helped me with my homework." As far as Wil and his teacher were concerned, father and son were both failing fractions. Wil thought it was a good time to talk about a painful subject, especially since Dad appeared to be in such an understanding mood.

My father sat there listening patiently for about twice as long as I'd expected him to. Wil took a deep breath in preparation of explaining just exactly why he and fractions didn't get along. He was about to go into his theory of why none of it was his fault, but I spoke before he could get fully started.

"Wil," I said as he started to explain why calculators made learning math unnecessary, "Daddy wants

21

to know what you meant when you asked him about calling someone else Daddy. He wants to know if Mama has a boyfriend." That was a topic of conversation that came up with my mother as well. Of course she never wanted to know if Daddy had a boyfriend. Her interest was whether or not he ever invited "someone else," such as another female, to dinner with us. After asking that, she'd always go into her speech about how she was our mother, our first-and-last and one-and-only mother. We knew that one by heart, too.

"Oh, that," Wil said and slurped the dregs of his piña colada through a tiny bar straw.

"Yes, the jackpot question, brother dear."

"I wouldn't exactly put it that way," Daddy said, still keeping his voice level and calm, then scratching his thumb, touching his nose, and rubbing his ear. He went on to explain that all he was really interested in was my mother's happiness, and how if she found someone to make her happy, that would make him happy. But he certainly didn't look happy. He looked even less happy when Wil mentioned Albert.

"Albert!" my father boomed so loudly that the man in the next booth almost jumped out of his seat. Daddy knew Albert, of course. We all knew Albert. He'd gone to law school with my mother and worked in an office right near hers. He'd even come to visit us the first, last, and only time we'd rented a house in the country for the summer. He stayed two weeks.

Everybody in the restaurant was staring at us, and Daddy looked embarrassed. He adjusted his tie and pulled one shirt cuff so hard it reached his knuckles. "Albert!" he said in a loud whisper. And then he said it was possible that our mother had completely lost her mind. "She must be crazy!" he boomed again, and the people in the next booth got up hurriedly and left. Daddy took his reading glasses out, cleaned them, and put them away.

"Daddy," I said calmly, "Albert isn't exactly Mama's boyfriend." I knew this to be a fact, because when I'd asked Mama if Albert was her boyfriend, she said that Albert was a friend of hers who happened to be a boy. That is, she added, he was a friend of hers who used to be a boy, and now he was a man who was a friend of hers. So my mother had a manfriend. Somehow that sounded worse, so I didn't mention it to Daddy. He'd get all excited again, and in a way, I couldn't blame him. They weren't even divorced, and here was my mother with a manfriend. It almost sounded like bigamy! But I didn't mention that either. I told my father that Albert and my mother were just friends who liked to go to dinner together.

I asked Daddy if he had a girlfriend, or a friend who used to be a girl who was now a woman. First he said I was too young to be concerned with such things. Then he said no and looked at his watch. "Are you sure?" I asked. "After all, there must be someone you like to have dinner with sometimes." He said that was the kind of talk he wanted to have with me sometime in the future—and looked at his watch. "It's totally beside the point. We're talking here about a newly separated female, unsure, confused, not intellectually prepared to cope with her new status."

"Is he talking about Mama?" Wil wanted to know.

"Daddy," I reminded him, "you've always told us how smart Mama is, and clearheaded."

"Yes, yes, you're right. Your mother is all those things. But who knows what's going on in her mind these days. She could be under a strain," he said. Then he offered to explain the psychological aspects of

23

my mother's situation. Mama had already explained her legal rights to us. Daddy took out a pen and pad in order to draw us a chart. Wil laid his head down on the table, and I pretended to doze off in a seated position.

"All right," he said, "I won't explain the psychological aspects of the situation." He looked just a bit put out. I imagine he had some really fine jargon to toss at us, and by this time his calculator was on the table and he seemed a little disappointed at not getting to use it, as he loves statistics. Mama is a whiz with legal phrases. "Does she look to you kids as if she's under a strain?" he asked. "How about it, Wil, how does she look? Let's say on a scale of one to ten."

Wil raised his head and thought about it for a moment. "I'd rather put it in words," he said. Daddy quickly put his calculator away and laid down his pen. He returned the pad to his inside pocket. I woke up for his answer. "She looks kind of—" Wil said and hesitated. "Kind of—let me put it this way. She hums to herself a lot lately, and she's always smiling except when she mentions you, and well, I guess she looks kind of—happy."

That's all Daddy ever told us he wanted her to be—happy. Now we were telling him that she was just as he wished she was—happy. You would think that would have made him happy. Instead, he clutched his stomach and made a low rumbling sound, something like a volcano that's about to erupt.

Wil asked if he could have another piña colada, and Daddy said *"No!"* so loudly that everybody in the restaurant jumped.

We walked home slowly. It had just started to drizzle slightly, a spring city rain that kind of misted down. It made the streets and the leaves on the trees smell green and fresh. We all held hands. When we got back to our building, I got Fluff from the car, and Daddy decided to come up, so I held Fluff in my arms. By now, the volcano in his stomach had subsided and cooled into a quiet, steady simmer. He insisted on ringing the bell before we walked in through the door, and when no one answered, he stuck his head inside the apartment and called out "Hello," as if we might be interrupting something. There was no answer, so he did it again with the same result. After waiting a few minutes, he allowed us all through the door. Once inside, I put Fluff in my bedroom. My father looked miserably at his armchair and then sadly at us. He began nonchalantly to wander some of the rooms, looking for some physical evidence of Albert's new status in our household. I don't know what he expected to find—a cigar butt, maybe? I don't even think Albert smokes cigars. I began to wish for Daddy's sake that his car was double-parked; I thought it would take his mind off his troubles.

About a half hour later, we heard the sound of the key in the lock and Mama walked in, quite alone. First my father looked almost disappointed. Then he tried looking casual and sat down in the fur-covered chair. My mother came into the living room, said hello to Wil and me, looked at Daddy, and said hello to him. She was trying to look casual, too. I think she knew that he knew about Albert.

If she did know that he knew, she acted as if she didn't know. But I think Daddy knew that she knew that he knew. They'd been married a long time, and in all those years I think they got to know each other. Mama didn't let any cats out of any bags. She brought up her favorite subject: getting the kids into camp for the summer.

"You'll need new riding boots," my mother said to me, and then she dropped the news that she and Albert and some other "singles," as she put it, were thinking of renting a house in Southampton for the summer. Daddy looked ill. Mama noticed it.

Then she said she felt ten years younger already.

Wil and I groaned when we heard that, because that's how she said she felt whenever Albert came to visit. She'd tell us about how she felt ten years younger. Wil and I were worried about it. After all, she was planning to spend the whole summer with him. By September, we might have an absolute infant on our hands.

"Why can't we spend the summer in Southampton with you?" I asked as a last desperate means of escaping the inevitable. "Wil and I are singles, and they must have horses in Southampton. Just think of all the money you'd save. I wouldn't have to buy a new footlocker, and I could wear my old boots."

Mama said I'd hate it.

They were both quick to agree I'd hate it. Daddy didn't want his children sleeping under the same roof with Albert and took lots of great pains to let Mama know how he felt about that. Mostly, he felt red in the face. He didn't shout or anything. The words just kind of smoldered out between his teeth. Mama was a little too quick to agree with him, I must say. Even Wil was surprised. We began to suspect another one of those foregone conclusions on the horizon.

"Wil and I will sleep in the garage. It does have a garage, doesn't it, Mama? And Daddy, Albert doesn't have a car. We wouldn't even be sleeping under the same roof with his automobile!"

Chapter Four

The day we went to camp was one of those special-arrangement situations. My parents couldn't decide which of them would drive us up there, so they both decided to go. Wil and I wanted to go in two cars, like a caravan, but at a special meeting called to inform us of our decision, we were told the plan of action. Daddy would drive, and Mama would navigate. Wil and I offered to take the bus.

That morning, I turned over in bed and woke up to the delicious aroma of breakfast cooking. Mama was scrambling a huge panful of eggs, and muffins were in the toaster. Wil came out of his room still asleep and walked like a zombie to the table. Generally, Mama only cooked breakfast when she expected to be away on business for a few days, but this morning Wil and I were the ones who were leaving, so Mama even squeezed oranges.

"Why don't you feed us like this all the time?" I asked her.

"Cereal is a perfectly healthy breakfast, Tiffin," she said extra gently, because I was going away. "It has vitamins, and roughage, and I always get the kind that has no artificial ingredients or preservatives."

She looked at my face a few minutes to see if I appreciated all the trouble she was going through for my roughage. I tried to look thankful, and I suppose I did. Mama reached across the table and gave my forearm a gentle, loving grip. Then she sighed happily about how perfect it all was, and I sighed about how perfect it all was, and Wil sighed, or he may have snored.

"How about some more eggs?" Mama asked me warmly when she got tired of looking at all the gratitude on my face. I really didn't want any more eggs; I'd had two helpings already. Mama wondered what she'd do with them all, and I suggested that Daddy might eat them. My mother agreed that he might, and she quickly gave them to Fluff—who certainly did eat them.

Daddy came up and rang the bell, so Mama jogged to the bathroom. Wil let him in, and I gave him a huge portion of my eggs. We sat around and sighed with him this time, until Wil burped and said, "'Scuse me." Then he went to his room to watch his Saturday-morning shows. I looked at my watch, and it was time to get out of pajamas and into some clothes for our trip. I thought about a last civilized shower till September and decided it was worth the detour. And I could listen to the waterproof wall radio Daddy gave Mama on New Year's Eve.

We left Daddy sitting, sighing, and facing a huge portion of Wil's eggs while Fluff stared at them both. Mama got dressed and went into the kitchen where she almost fainted when she saw who was eating her eggs. She quickly bustled Daddy up, out, and towards a growing pile of odd-size suitcases.

"Why didn't you send this stuff in the trunk last month?" he asked, attempting to lift a medium-size bag containing my thirty-pound supply of ceramics clay. There'd been no room in the trunk for it at all, so I'd put it in my strongest bag along with the books I absolutely promised myself I'd read this year. "If we pull together on this," my mother said to him in a patient, reasoning tone of voice, "we can get the job done and enjoy it as well. Now, come on," she encouraged. "You take these two bags to start with, and I'll hold the door open."

"Why," Daddy asked quietly, "don't you take these two bags to start with, and I'll hold the door open?"

Mama got a headache, and Daddy called Biff the doorman. When Biff saw the pile, he turned to my father and said, "You'll give me a hand here, won't you?"

Mama just smiled and felt better already. Daddy said something, no one could understand what, but I guess he agreed, because the next thing he knew he had a small bag in each hand. Luckily for him, one contained a few stuffed animals and my pillow. Unluckily for him, the other contained my LP record collection.

After they'd gotten the first load downstairs and outside, Daddy and the doorman decided how to proceed by flipping a coin. The way it worked out, Daddy went up and down with the luggage while Biff stood guard on the sidewalk. Then Biff continued his vigil while Daddy walked two blocks to get the car from the closest parking space he'd been able to find.

Daddy double-parked in front of our building and

told us urgently over the intercom to come downstairs while he packed the car. Then he and Biff moved the bags through the cars at the curb in a kind of a sideways shuffle between bumpers. They made a nice, orderly pile behind our car, and naturally half of it wouldn't fit into the trunk.

Daddy tried packing it a few different ways as Biff offered scientific suggestions about weight and mass (he was going to night school). Finally Daddy started to throw the baggage at the trunk, but Biff told him the basics of the theory of projectiles, and then Daddy started to throw it at the doorman. We arrived out front just in time to stop Daddy from launching my suitcase full of porcelain horses into the lobby. Daddy and Biff never really got along anyway. Before my folks split up, Biff always thought Daddy's Christmas present envelopes to him were too thin. Now, whenever Daddy came to the building, Biff stopped him at the intercom and asked whom he should announce.

Mama took charge of supervising the stowing operation so they wound up with a two-suiter between them in the front. Mama calculated that the drive should take under three hours, and we could all be a little inconvenienced for such a short time.

Wil and I were to share the back seat with our duffel bags, two rolled-up quilts, his boombox, my Walkman portable radio, and two sets of hopelessly tangled earphones.

When my father was finally finished "working like a slave," as he put it, he happily told us all to "pile in," but Wil said he'd forgotten something upstairs and sprinted into the lobby. He'd been gone about ten minutes when my mother remembered that she'd forgotten something upstairs, and she met Wil on his way out. She must have forgotten to take a nap or something, because she was up there a good half hour.

"How about you?" my father turned in his seat and asked me as my mother came out of the building. "You forget something, too?"

"No," I answered, "but I do have to go to the bathroom."

I wasn't gone long, considering that someone was using the elevator to move a piano. But it wasn't as if I was holding anything up; the doorman refused to move from in front of the car till Daddy gave him a better tip.

"Pay the doorman," my mother said calmly.

"Why don't you pay the doorman?" my father answered quietly. "He is, after all, your doorman."

Faced with that piece of logic, Mama got very stiff. Her face got stiff. Her voice got stiff. The way she moved and turned her head got stiff. She was very stiff until Daddy tipped the doorman, and Biff let us drive away before Daddy almost ran him over and Mama turned into a statue.

"You're going the wrong way," were her first un-stiffing words to him. On a ratio of one to ten, they were about an eight on the stiffness scale.

What then proceeded was a kind of hockey game where Mama would suggest an alternate route and Daddy would tell her what was wrong with it: "They're tearing up that street for two miles around," and things like that. Then he'd mutter something about Saturday traffic, or how today was the day everybody was taking kids to camp. Most of the kids must have been hidden out of sight. As far as I could see, we were the only people around sitting on duffel bags.

We left the city over the Triborough Bridge and

headed towards New England. When we were on the highway, Mama asked if we had enough gas, because she never thinks we have enough gas. Daddy said we had enough gas, because he always thinks we have enough gas. They spent almost an hour discussing the gas until Wil said he felt carsick.

Wil never gets carsick. He just feels carsick. It generally happens in the vicinity of brightly lit rest stops with french fries. And it doesn't go away until he gets some.

"Pull into the next plaza," my mother said urgently, relieved that now we could get gas.

Daddy turned on his directional signal as we left the highway, as, so it seemed, had everybody else on the road. There were no parking spaces in front of the restaurant. It must have been all those people taking all those kids to camp.

Wil and I went in first, and Daddy said he'd get gas and by then there'd be a space. Mama took her briefcase from the car and found us three seats at the counter. Wil ordered his french fries, I had a vanilla malted, and Mama ordered coffee and a blueberry muffin.

"I didn't know you liked blueberry muffins," I said and thought it was interesting that even after all this time, there were still things I didn't know about her.

"I don't really. They're all right, I suppose."

"Then why did you order it?" Was this a mystery? Was she ordering a blueberry muffin at a rest stop as some sentimental reminder of a former time? Do you suppose it was Daddy? I wonder what he looked like then. Was this the place? On the other hand, was she now going to share some awful secret that might change my life? I braced myself for the answer and found that I was breathing a little more quickly.

"One of our clients is being sued for leaving the blueberries out of his muffins."

"Why would he do that?" I asked as we both watched the waitress present the specimen like an offering on a plate.

"Well, he says he didn't. He says three berries to the muffin is an industry standard. So everywhere I go," she said and began to slice the muffin into thin slivers, "I order a muffin and look for blueberries. Aha!" she said as she found one and lifted it gently out of the dough with the tip of her butter knife. "That way," she said, holding up the purple squoosh for closer inspection, "I get to write this off as a business expense, and I can charge my hourly fee."

"In that case," said Wil, "I'll have another order of french fries."

Mama completed her investigation into the contents of the muffin, and judging from the pile on the plate, she'd found a manufacturer who exceeded industry standards for blueberries. Mama took her calendar book out of her briefcase and made a note of the time she'd spent on the case. She drank her coffee, looked around the even-more-crowded restaurant for a sign of Daddy, and asked the waitress for the check.

"Should we get Daddy some coffee?" I asked.

"He probably already got some," she answered. "And you know how cranky too much coffee makes him."

I wasn't sure about that. But I did know how cranky too little coffee made him.

We got outside and there was Daddy circling the restaurant, waving and calling to us from his window while a state trooper kept the traffic moving. He was allowed to stop and pick us up, and the first question he asked Mama was whether she had gotten him coffee.

"Why? Are you falling asleep at the wheel?" she asked, studying him carefully for signs of drowsiness.

"You didn't get me coffee?"

Mama didn't get a chance to answer. Wil said he felt carsick, and we had to go speeding off to the next rest stop.

The car's engine began to overheat shortly after our fourth stop. It isn't exactly the latest model. Daddy's had it for years and refuses to give it up. He says that at least it's paid for, and that's more than most cars can say. It makes steam too, and that's more than most cars can do. By the time we growled up to the service area, it was making huge billows of it. We came to a stop like a locomotive, with great blasts of white vapor settling nicely on the windshield.

We went into the coffee shop, and Mama dissected her fifth muffin of the day while Daddy and the mechanic waited for the radiator to cool. Mama finished her work, and I think she decided that her client was in trouble. She put her notebook away, pushed the plate of muffin shards out of her sight, and said that tests like this were hardly conclusive evidence.

As for the car, it needed a new radiator hose that the mechanic did not have. He wrapped the leak with black tape but suggested that we stop in the next town and have it replaced. He said there was a large garage a stone's throw from the highway. Well the stones there must have wings, because it was almost dark by the time we found the place, and the owner wanted to go home.

We all tried to look pitiful so he'd fix the car, but he checked out our luggage and Mama's briefcase and decided that we weren't as humble as we looked. As far as he was concerned, we were city folks touring the world in an old car to fool the natives. He charged us accordingly and took over two hours to do it.

When it was finally fixed, Daddy got back behind the wheel. He'd been holding the service light so the garage owner could see what he was doing—what he does when Daddy's not around is hard to say. Mama was just waiting for my father to mention how much it cost, so she could say, "It's your car," in the same tone of voice he'd said, "It's your doorman." Somehow I think he knew what was waiting, and he didn't say a word. If you knew my father, you'd know how unusual that was.

The man gave us explicit directions on how to get back to the highway. We followed them right up until we got lost. It was very dark by then, and it looked like Wil and I would be starting our first day at camp in the middle of the night. Wil sensed the opportunity to spend a night in a motel—one of his favorite passions—and he began to yawn loudly. Mama remembered that one of her clients was being sued for giving less than a minute for a quarter on a vibrating bed. We could check in, and she could work on the case.

"Pull in here," she commanded at the sight of a sign calling *Welcome* and *Comforts*. Daddy growled something, or he may have just growled, but we drove into the parking lot and came to a stop in front of the lobby.

Daddy looked quickly into his rearview mirror. "Now listen," he said, getting suddenly excited, "don't anyone get excited."

"No vacancies?" I asked.

"It's not that," my father said tensely. "I think we're being followed. I noticed it at our fourth rest stop. Don't anyone turn around and look at the car," he ordered urgently. So naturally we all turned around and looked at the car.

"Oh," my mother said lightly, "that's just Albert."

"Albert!" My father turned around and looked at the car.

"Yes," said my mother, ever patient. "Albert and Fluff."

"Albert and Fluff!" my father said, looking at the car again. Then he looked at me. "You see!" he said, referring to my Southampton garage offer. "He does have a car."

"It's rented," my mother explained reasonably. "And please calm down. You know how it makes Wil sick."

"What, may I ask," my father asked in a hoarse whisper that sounded loud even though it was low, "are your—your—boyfriend and your—your—rabid dog doing here?" I thought he was going to fall right out of the car. Then he reminded himself that he was a psychologist and made a deep-breathing effort to calm down. That's what he does whenever he reminds himself he's a psychologist. Deep breathing must be one of the first things they learn.

My mother said that first of all, Albert was not her boyfriend. He was her lawyer. Her lawyer. Well, I thought, that was different. That made it all right. But my father didn't think so and offered to tell my mother her unconscious motivations. She said she could have used that information a long time ago, on the day they got married.

"Because goodness knows," she said sharply, "I must have been unconscious at the time."

This signaled the start of their who-proposed-to-whom discussion. Then Mama said it was all Daddy's fault, anyway. Albert eats at the same Chinese restaurant as we do, and he'd heard all about my father's bizarre behavior and had come along in case Mama needed someone to call for help. Besides, she pointed out, she intended to drive to Southampton with Albert to look at houses.

"You mean you're not driving back with me?" my father asked incredulously.

"I drove up here with you," my mother answered stiffly. Then she got out of the car and went to register, so Wil and I went to say hello to Fluff. Albert was attempting to get out of his car, but Fluff didn't want him to go. She likes him, mainly I think because he lets her chew on his ties without making a fuss about it.

Mama came out of the office and instructed Daddy which suitcases were needed for the night. We left Fluff running around the shrubbery and joined them.

"Hello Sam," Albert said.

"Hello Albert," my father said.

"Miffie," Albert said to my mother, "I thought this place was three hours away."

Daddy stiffened a little when he heard Albert call Mama *Miffie*. We all stiffened a little, I think. All except Mama, who didn't seem to notice. Then Daddy asked about the "sleeping arrangements." Mama said she didn't know what his plans were, but as for her and her children, they had a room with twin double beds and a color television.

"Plus," she added, "each room has its own little individual coffee maker."

Hearing that, Albert dashed into the office to register. He came back just as the sign over Daddy's head lit up with a huge NO in front of the VACANCY.

Daddy looked at the sign, looked at Albert, and said, "See here, Albert."

37

And Albert said, dangling the key to the last room, "It's a single."

It's a good thing we had those quilts in the back of the car all rolled up like that. Not that he would need them in that early summer weather, but the thought seemed comforting just the same. We lent Daddy a pillow from Wil's double bed and turned up the air-conditioning. Daddy went back to the car, moved the suitcase that shared the front seat, opened up all the windows, and attempted to stretch out on the front seat. Somewhere, secretly, he was glad, I think. Because he knew Mama would give him a cup of coffee in the morning and let him use our bathroom—and he would have saved all that money on a room. That thought brought a silent smile to his face as he drifted off to sleep.

"Fluff!" Albert called out his door before retiring for the night. *"Fluff!"*

Daddy bolted awake in the front seat and got his foot caught in the steering wheel.

"Fluff!" Albert called.

"Quiet!" Daddy called back.

"I think she's lost," Albert said in a hoarse whisper.

"Good!" Daddy whispered back and rearranged himself again.

Fluff wasn't lost, of course. She was just exploring her first motel. She came back looking for us, probably going from door to door and deciding that we were asleep. Then she jumped into our car through the open front window and danced on Daddy all night.

Chapter Five

The next morning we found Daddy asleep on the grass beside the car. Fluff was behind the steering wheel with all the windows rolled to within two inches of the top. She was standing on the seat with her paws near the horn and was able to show her teeth through the opening while she growled playfully but steadily at my father.

Albert came out and surveyed the scene and asked Daddy if he'd been drinking rum again. Daddy told Albert to go away, and Mama brought out a cup of coffee. When my father finally did get up and brush himself off, his clothing fit him like a crumpled tissue. He stumbled to the room and fell asleep in the shower. Afterwards, he stumbled to the car—which my mother insisted on driving. Then he fell asleep during the rest of the ride to camp. It's too bad, because he was missing some very pretty scenery. The back-country was still lit with dew on the leaves. The cows barely raised their heads as we drove by. Some of them were lying down, meaning that it either was or wasn't going to rain.

Suddenly a huge wooden totem pole appeared on the right-hand side of the road announcing that we had indeed arrived. Mama woke Daddy up when we got there. He was supposed to help with the luggage. He got out of the car and walked so woozily with the bags that we wound up making two trips to his one, although he covered more ground. Still, Albert didn't approve of that at all, but Daddy ignored him and then fell asleep on my cot just before my counselor walked in to introduce herself.

"How do you do?" Daddy said sleepily, rising from his nap to be polite. "Nicetohavemetyou," he added and staggered out the door in search of our car.

Serena, my counselor, looked at me with a lot of sympathy. Then she left to tell everybody she could find about it. As she went out the door, she called to me over her shoulder, "By the way, you know you're a day late." As if I couldn't tell. As if I didn't know. "All the good bunks are gone."

Somehow, I had landed in a bunk house that looked like something out of a black-and-white movie about Tarzan. There were four doddering cots under equally ancient warped windows. Naturally, being the last girl to arrive—and on the second day, too—I got the bed nearest the screen with a hole in it. I looked out at my view and got an unobstructed study of a big blue bug zapper hanging from the trees. Hopefully its neon light would lure the mosquitoes away from my direction. For that little privilege, I got to listen to the hiss of insects meeting their doom.

Anyway, I thought, I'd have my own horse for the summer. And Wil would have his soccer. But what would Mama and my father have? I wondered whether my parents could handle being left on their own for two months. What if one of them got married? What if they both got married? What if they got divorced?

If they did, I supposed, life would somehow go on. I'd have two rooms, and two allowances, and two people ready to do the opposite of what the other threatened. Things could be worse, I thought. After all, I knew enough people in the same circumstances. I didn't feel that my whole world was about to crumble. I didn't even feel that I was about to come from a broken home. It didn't seem as much broken as extended. My home now extended to two apartments.

If anything, the way things were working out, I was seeing both my parents more now than I did when we were one big happy family sharing one place to live.

The quality of the time we spent together was different, too. Before, I saw Daddy in the morning while he waited for someone to come out of the bathroom so he could shave. Now, he was always perfectly groomed and we were seeing him in the best restaurants. Before, Mama was someone who left after cereal and came back before hamburgers. Now, she took Wil and me to the movies and sometimes the theater. All in all, besides sometimes being plunked into the middle of their who-was-to-blame theories, it wasn't as awful an experience as the movies made it. I wasn't about to start wearing tight red skirts and whistling at sailors or anything like that. I didn't intend to take drugs, drink alcohol, or become a behavioral problem at school. I'm not saying that I felt, let's say, carefree. I felt concerns; who wouldn't? Part of it was the possibility of stepparents. After all, look what happened to Hänsel and Gretel. But Daddy swore solemnly that once single, he would stay single forever. But that was after Wil had three piña coladas in the Chinese restaurant one night.

Mama hugged us one day and told us she already had all the family she needed, and she hugged us again. But a friend of mine from school has gone through this sort of thing twice! She said that these feelings on the part of my parents were just a stage they were going through. She said that in no time at all they'd be behaving like teenagers, and I should be prepared.

Right then, what I had to worry about was making up my camp bed. Would the sheets fit? Would the mattress have lumps? The answer to both was yes. I opened my first-night suitcase, even though it would be my second night, and found my first-night snack pack. In honor of the occasion, and with mixed feelings about most things in general, I ate the cookies. I sat on my bed and felt the way I imagine a prisoner of war feels the first day in captivity. I'd be there for two months, and the prospect of watching my parents leave in two different cars was a little more than I wanted to deal with just then.

Mama came into the bunk house with Mr. Hildebrande, the owner of the camp. She introduced us, and we shook hands, and he remarked that he'd just met Daddy. Then he looked at me with raised eyebrows and nodded kindly at Mama.

Albert, on the other hand, was standing outside near his car being treated like visiting royalty by campers and counselors alike. After seeing Daddy walking in his sleep and napping all over the place while Albert toted, everyone was going out of her way to shake Albert's hand and offer him encouraging pats on the back.

Inside, Mr. Hildebrande whispered confidentially that he liked my stepfather! I whispered back that he was my mother's lawyer, and he said, "Oh."

Mama happened to mention to me that she'd have to be leaving soon to go to Southampton. Then Mr. Hildebrande asked her why she was going to Southampton, as he used to run a camp there. She told him about renting a house, and his eyes lit up like an electric cash register.

Mr. Hildebrande, as it happened, owned several houses surrounding Camp Chucalucup that he rented to the same families every summer. He also traded horses, sold insurance, and took magazine orders.

This summer it seemed one of the families who'd rented there for years had to cancel their arrangements at the last minute.

"Naturally," Mr. Hildebrande said regretfully, "they lost their deposit." Then he indicated a bargain might be available to the right party, and he looked very appraisingly at Mama, who looked back at him in her best courtroom style.

He took Mama by the arm and led her out the door, down the drive, and across the road. I just followed the real-estate tour.

We stopped in front of a small white Victorian house that had an even smaller studio cottage behind the huge rear lawn. Mr. Hildebrande showed Mama around while he listed all the cultural activities the area offered—concerts, summer stock, swimming, boating, gardening.

When he said *gardening,* my mother echoed "gardening" in a wistful way that made me wonder when she'd gotten dreamy about gardening. Maybe this was another thing I was learning about her up close and personal. Maybe gardens were something deeply

43

meaningful to her, even though I never even saw her walk in the dirt, let alone dig in it. Then Mr. Hildebrande mentioned the weekly horse show she could watch me ride in, and he quoted her a rental price that was roughly one-half of what she expected to have to pay for just a share in a house in Southampton.

Mr. Hildebrande confided to her a series of highway numbers that were guaranteed to get her from door to door in under two hours and twenty-two minutes.

Mama looked at me and said, "The horse shows sound lovely," and she smiled tenderly. "And I'd be near my children," she said, looking to see if I appreciated the sentiment. In fact, I did. There's nothing like weekend dinners away from camp. And right across the road, too. Then Mama mentioned one of the several four-week vacations she never took, looked around the bright little house, and began to calculate.

For one thing, since she'd be renting the whole house, she could invite important clients for summer weekends in the country. There would be the excitement and diversion of the weekly horse show to keep them entertained; there would be fresh salads from the garden; and she could write the whole thing off as a legitimate business expense. She inspected the three small bedrooms: one to be hers, one a guest room, and the third to be used as an office for getting some work done on those long-weekend Mondays.

"This will do nicely," she said after inspecting the cozy dining room, and she reached for her checkbook. I was happy to see her looking so happy. After all, it was a triumph for her. It not only satisfied her love of a bargain and helped soothe her slight feelings of guilt, it made good business sense besides.

Mr. Hildebrande beamed and said I should show up

for camp that day anytime that I wanted to. He said all the good horses were taken anyway. Then he winked and did a few steps in a jig of delight and left us in Mama's new house. It was an interesting experience for me, too. Mama saw, she liked, and she rented. She was a person in her own right, making her own choices, with her own money, and her own motivations. She was as close to being exhilarated as I've ever known her to be. I was happy to have witnessed this joy of independence on her part.

We sat down at the sunlit kitchen table while she made a list of things she'd have to buy—coffee, sugar, napkins, and other summer-house things like that. It seemed to me that she was starting to have a lot of fun already.

I explored the house while Mama drove our car up to the front drive with Daddy still asleep in the back seat. She came back into the house carrying her small Southampton suitcase, and I helped her choose the best bedroom.

I leaned out the window and called to Daddy in our car. Albert was standing across the road still making friends. He saw me and shouted, "Hallo."

Daddy woke up and peered out over the car windows. When he came indoors to find us, Mama told him what was going on, and she was very fair about it, too. She offered to sublet the studio cottage to him for about the price she was paying for the whole place.

That offer had the effect it always has when Mama talks to Daddy about money. He stumbled backwards and groped around behind him for a chair. Then he sat down heavily and looked betrayed. He offered to swap his professional services in lieu of rent. He said that in exchange for the cottage, he would tell Mama what was wrong with her.

He said she'd rented the house on purpose, and she agreed. Daddy said she knew very well that he was too cheap to pay to live in more than one place at a time. He said that as her husband, he was practically entitled to the studio cottage. He offered to drive her up and back on weekends in exchange for it and half the cost of the gas.

Mama took legal exception to everything he said. She explained the laws of separation and of leases, and specified cash, but added that she'd take a check, reluctantly. She told him she intended to lease a car. "A nice, air-conditioned, reliable car," she added with a smile.

Daddy smiled back. It was one of his sardonic smiles, which generally means he's about to deliver a devastating psychological insight in Mama's direction.

"You'll see," he said, nodding his head in agreement. "A couple of days out in the country alone, life in the rough..." He went on as if the house didn't have lights, heat, or running water. "You'll beg me to use the studio. And then," he said, folding his arms in front of his chest like an Indian chief surveying his wigwams, "just maybe, you'll have to ask twice. If," he said, "you don't ask now."

He and Mama stared at each other while he waited for her to pop the question.

"That reminds me," my mother said and sat down at the table in front of her list. "I don't want to forget flour," she said and penciled it in. "I just feel a need to bake bread."

"You see," my father said, "it's starting already. Baking bread is always the first sign. Soon you'll be chopping wood. I'll tell you what, the use of that cottage will entitle you to fifteen—no, twenty—hours of in-depth analysis."

"Cash," said Mama.

"All right then—twenty-five hours, but you have to pay for all the gas. It's only right; think how much you'll save by not leasing a car." But Mama stayed silent and added to her shopping list. Daddy watched her awhile and said he'd let her think it over. "There's no hurry," he added, turning slowly, about to stalk majestically out of the room.

Just then Albert came in and Mama offered him the rental of the studio cottage on the same terms. She told him what Mr. Hildebrande had said about the attractions of the area. Albert hurried to the cottage for a brief inspection of the premises and hurried right back to accept then and there. He even paid a deposit in cash. Not only was Mama getting a business deduction, she was operating at a profit. I came away very impressed with her ability to function all alone in the world except for me and Wil.

I think Daddy was impressed, too. He went to the nearest town and bought a canopied sleeping bag that he set up on the lawn between the two houses.

Chapter Six

Mama looked at me looking at her guest room and asked me why I wasn't in camp. I told her about the torn screen and all the good horses being gone, and she told me how much camp was costing us. So, reluctantly, I crossed the road and went to my bunk house.

My roommates were there, wondering who belonged to the pile of stuff on my bed. We introduced ourselves, and they told me I was late and had missed out on everything. Then Lily, the girl who slept opposite me, clutched her hands over her chest and announced dramatically, "This could be it."

"Oh please," Jennifer groaned, "not again."

Lily and Jennifer were second-year campers and had roomed together before. "I lived through all this with you last year, Lily," she said, scraping mud off her field boots. "Have mercy, please."

"You mean," Joan, a new camper just like me,

asked Lily, "you're not going to grow right before our very eyes? I'm disappointed."

"So is she," Jennifer said. "Last summer she checked herself out in the mirror every morning."

"There's nothing wrong with being prepared," Lily protested. "It can happen practically overnight. My mother says so."

"That's what you said last summer, Lily. Tell me, why is it so important for you to develop a bust?"

"Because of this," Lily said and reached deep into her footlocker. She groped around a few minutes, digging deeper and deeper through her packed clothing. Finally she seemed to find what she was looking for. "Aha!" she shouted in triumph, dangling a tiger-skin print brassiere in front of our faces.

"I can't believe it," Jennifer laughed. "You're still carting that thing around with you?"

Lily held it closer to Joan and me so we could get a better look at her treasure.

"It's Swedish," Lily sighed, looking lovingly at her precious possession. "And I get to wear it as soon as I grow into it."

"I hate to tell you this, dear friend"—Jennifer smiled—"but it'll be years before you need that little number."

"I'll be wearing it before summer's over, just you wait and see," Lily sniffed haughtily, stuffing her lingerie back into the bottom of her trunk.

"Can everybody keep a secret?" Joan asked, looking at us one at a time. Then she opened her footlocker and reached inside.

Jennifer looked up from her boots. "Don't tell us that you've got some fancy Swedish undies, too?"

"No." Joan laughed. "But I do have this." She took

out a battery-operated television set with a five-inch screen.

"We're saved," I shouted, taking out one of the care packages Wil and I had spent a month putting together. "Gummy bears, anybody?"

Needless to say, everybody wanted gummy bears, and the reception on the television was snowy but comforting. We watched until dinnertime, then we went to the mess hall. We lined up with our trays and waited our turn to get turkey chunks and gravy. I say chunks because it looked like the meat had been torn off the turkey with the cook's bare hands.

Then someone said that the cook was an escaped criminal who'd poisoned the potato salad at his last job. Naturally, that information gave everybody a real appetite, and I wondered how long I could exist on gummy bears. Lily said I should ignore the rumors about the cook. She said they were started by Mr. Hildebrande in an attempt to get the campers to eat less.

Jennifer agreed. "Last year, he said that showering with warm water weakened the mind. I guess this year he just wants to save on food."

I felt a little reassured. Even so, a lot of people at the table were waiting for the person next to them to take the first bite—and nobody would even touch the potato salad with her fork.

On our way back from dinner, Lily clutched her stomach and asked what the symptoms of ptomaine poisoning were.

"If you're dead in the morning, we'll know you had it," Joan said kindly.

"I'll give you the gummy bear antidote," I offered, and we scampered into our bunk house only to discover that someone had frenched our sheets.

"Oh no," moaned Jennifer, "don't tell me that Serena's our counselor again."

Lily sat down hard on her bed. "I don't know if I can handle another summer coping with her. Especially not when my chest is growing and I'm suffering from ptomaine at the same time."

"She was in here before," I said. "She seemed very nice."

"You mean, you've been here for less than a day and you actually saw Serena?" Jennifer asked in amazement. "I was here five weeks last year before I ever laid eyes on her."

"I don't think I ever met her," Lily said, deep in attempted recollection. "Sometimes I used to think she was a myth."

Serena was real all right. She just stayed out of sight most of the time. Out of our sight anyway. The story was that there was a shack in the woods from which certain counselors hardly ever emerged. Serena was one of them. When she did come out to check up on her wards for the season, she liked to leave evidence of her concern. Today it was frenched sheets. Jennifer warned us that in the long days that would follow, we could expect frogs in our underwear and slugs in our shoes.

"I just hope she doesn't hose down the room again this year," Lily moaned. "Last year, my mattress didn't dry out until the third week in August. Do you know what it's like to spend your summer in a soppy bunk? I felt like a person with a terminal bed-wetting problem."

The next day I felt better than the day before. I woke up and asked Lily how things were developing. "Did anything happen during the night?"

"Verry funny Tin, verry, verry, funny!" she replied.

They had taken to calling me "Tin" because of my funny name and my new braces.

Jennifer sleepily swung her feet out of bed and plopped them straight into a pan of cold water half hidden on the floor beside her bunk.

"Yikes," she said and was wide awake already. She looked down at her free footbath and said a word or two she'd seen on a rest room wall.

"Serena strikes again," Lily said with a laugh. I have to admit that it was funny to see Jennifer's eyes pop open like that. She got up and threw the pan and water both out the front door. Lily continued to giggle until Jennifer took a pink brassiere out of her locker and put it on.

"Since when do you wear one of those?" Lily asked, sounding just a little bit jealous.

"Since I stuck my feet in the water," Jennifer answered a little sarcastically. "You should try it. It worked wonders for me."

Joan rolled over in bed and asked us to please carry on our conversation outside. "It's still the middle of the night," she said, yawning, and turned towards the wall.

"You'll miss breakfast, Joan," I told her.

"Somebody said there's arsenic in the oatmeal," she mumbled. Then, with her eyes still shut, she gathered her blanket snugly around her and in a minute was fast asleep.

I looked at the floor beneath my bed and then carefully poked my feet out of my quilt. I dressed in my camp shirt and my favorite tan breeches with genuine suede patches, pulled on my boots, and headed for the mess hall with Lily and Jen.

When we got to the building that housed the dining

room, there was a large crowd of campers standing out front and everybody was talking at once.

"What do you suppose is going on?" Lily wondered out loud.

"Maybe the oatmeal does have arsenic in it!" I said, suddenly worried about how I was going to make it through three meals a day.

Jen called to one of the kids she knew from last year.

"Hey Stockden," she shouted above the chatter, "what's going on?"

"They found a prowler last night," the girl answered breathlessly.

I looked at Jennifer. "Maybe that's who put the pan of water under your bed."

"What was he doing?" Lily asked.

"He was asleep in the field," Stockden whispered urgently, and I clutched my stomach. "Mr. Hildebrande's German shepherd chased him all over the camp. They're in the mess hall now."

"Asleep in the field?" Lily said, a little disappointed. "That doesn't sound like much of a prowler to me."

"It sounds like my father to me," I murmured.

"Your father's a prowler?" Lily asked, sounding shocked.

"Not exactly," I said. "He's a cheapskate."

Just then, the doors of the mess hall swung open and all the campers took a sudden step back. First, Mr. Hildebrande's German shepherd came out and barked at everybody, so everybody barked back. Then, Mr. Hildebrande appeared. He had his arm around my father's shoulder as if they were long-lost cousins. My father tried to smile to show everyone that everything was all right, but he was so tired by this time that his lips just curved up and down in different places—and everybody took another step back.

"Is there something wrong with him?" Jen whispered in my ear.

"He hasn't slept in two days," I said and went to help him down the stairs. He and Mr. Hildebrande were getting along famously. Mr. Hildebrande thought that Daddy was an avid outdoorsman and sold him a quart of musk-oil mosquito repellent. He also rented him the weekend use of a sleeping platform in a tree over the lake. It was a little rickety and just large enough for a sleeping bag, and Mr. Hildebrande assured Daddy that his dog couldn't climb trees.

My father was very happy with the deal too, as no cash had changed hands—except for the musk oil. In exchange for the sleeping accommodations, Daddy bartered his services as the camp's consulting psychologist so that Mr. Hildebrande could say he had one in his advertisements. In exchange for breakfasts, my father agreed to advise Mr. Hildebrande on when it was the right time, psychologically, to build condos on the property.

"Daddy," I said, taking his arm, "what happened?"

He studied my face a moment blearily. "Hello, dear," he said, because I think he couldn't remember my name. "Nothing happened. I just spent the night running through the woods in front of a crazed dog."

"I think he's drunk," Lily whispered to Jen. "Poor Tin."

"How do you feel?" I asked him.

"How do I look?" he asked back.

"Well," I hesitated, "if you really want to know, you look awful."

"That's how I feel," he said.

Mr. Hildebrande smiled benevolently at me. It wasn't every day that he got to do so much business with just one family. I think he was calculating how much a camp with its own consulting psychologist could charge for the second half of the season. He offered to show Daddy his new sleeping accommodations, and the two of them went off preceded by the barking dog. Mr. Hildebrande looked happy; my father looked wobbly.

"Have a nice breakfast," Daddy called to me sleepily over his shoulder.

"Try the oatmeal," Mr. Hildebrande shouted.

"You see!" warned Lily. "There is something wrong with it. Look what it did to your father!"

We all went in to breakfast, and following tradition, stopped first in front of Mr. Hildebrande's leather armchair to say good morning as if he were sitting there. Naturally, nobody tried the oatmeal—not in the whole camp. We all had eggs and last night's fried potatoes until the cook came out of the kitchen holding a large wooden spoon. He looked at the giant pot full of untouched oatmeal, banged his spoon against the wall for attention, and announced that if "the porridge," as he called it, wasn't gone before the end of breakfast, we were going to have it for lunch. His announcement was followed by groans, hoots, howls, and home fries tossed in his direction. Some of the kids had their riding crops, and it seemed that if you took a chunk of potato and held it in the loop at the tip of the crop, you could bend and launch the missile like a catapult.

"You'll see," he warned as he parried the potatoes with his wooden spoon. "You'll see," he shouted again as he retreated into the kitchen.

"He means it, too," Jen said sadly. "Last year he

served the same pot full of what he called spaghetti for almost a week."

"He would have served it a month," Lily added, "except somebody called the Board of Health."

We all looked glumly at the cauldron of oatmeal. Then a hero emerged from out of the crowd. It was our phantom counselor, Serena. She marched up to the counter, took the pot by both handles, and struggled with her burden towards Mr. Hildebrande's leather chair. She put the pot down, removed the seat cushion, and poured the oatmeal into the springs. Then she replaced the cushion, returned the pot, and disappeared into the crowd as quickly as she had come. Everyone was stunned, then everyone cheered, then everyone filed out of the dining hall, wondering what lunch would bring.

Chapter Seven

The morning was clear and cool and everyone applauded as Serena broke from the throng outside the dining hall and headed for her cabin in the woods. I was happy she'd gotten rid of the oatmeal in some place other than our beds. Lily told me not to worry. Serena had her own line, which she never crossed.

"She never does anything to her campers that will leave permanent scars or damage us emotionally," she explained carefully. I wasn't sure whether this was good news or not, but from her happy attitude, I guessed that it was. "And," she added, "she's a great rider." That relaxed me a little, as I always believed that anyone who is a great rider can't be all bad. Of course, I was willing to admit that perhaps certain people who were probably great riders might have had their own little idiosyncrasies—like Attila the Hun, for instance, or Sitting Bull, or even, for that matter, General Custer. But at least, I thought, if I ever met any of those great riders, we could always talk about horses. Keeping that in mind, I was prepared to give my counselor the benefit of the doubt. Especially since I had no other choice.

"Who are you riding?" Jen asked me as we walked up the hill towards the stable.

"I don't know yet," I told her. "I got here late, so I have to see what's left."

"Not much," Lily said. "I think no one took Demon."

"I'm not surprised," Jen laughed. "He got his name from running his riders into trees. Whatever you do, don't take Demon."

That sounded like good advice to me. Who wanted to spend the summer on a horse called Demon, especially if that meant sideswiping every tree in nature.

"And don't take Solitaire," Lily added urgently.

"But Solitaire is such a nice name," I said, repeating it to myself. Solitaire. It sounded romantic.

"Yes, and do you know why they call him Solitaire?" Jen asked me. "Because he always comes back alone."

"I think Mr. Hildebrande bought him from a rodeo," Lily said seriously. "Last year he kicked down his stall and was missing for three days."

"Well then," I asked, "who does that leave?"

My friends looked at each other and giggled. Then they looked at me and said, "Blue." And they giggled again.

"What happened to all those gorgeous horses they showed in the videotape?" I protested. "They can't all have been taken!"

"Ah, the videotape," they said together and began to laugh again. "This poor child saw the videotape." Lily consoled and patted me gently on the back. "Yes," she said, as if off in the memory, "I remember when I was that naive, too."

"It seems like years ago," Jen agreed. "I saw that tape last season. It all looked very nice. Mr. Hildebrande took the pictures himself, during the invitational horse show two years ago."

"You mean," I asked, flabbergasted, "that it's not true?"

"Let's just say it's exaggerated," Jennifer said gently.

"Just slightly," agreed Lily. "You remember all those horses who won the ribbons in the video?"

"You mean they didn't!" I was astonished.

"Oh they did all right; they won again last year, too. But they're all from outside contestants," Jen explained.

"All except Serena," Lily added quickly. "She has her own horse."

"That's why they put up with, let's say, her lack of application to duty," Jen explained.

"They need at least one ribbon winner on the staff, not to mention in the whole camp," Lily added. "It gives the place a little class." Then they both laughed as if it were the most jolly set of circumstances in the whole wide world.

I thought they were going to start rolling around on the ground. Lily said the nickname of my home for the next two months was Camp Off-the-Wall. Just what I needed! I had my own problems going for me. What with my parents' state of matrimony, and my father running around the woods with a dog all night, and tongues already beginning to wag over just exactly who Albert was and what he was doing there, I wasn't sure that I was prepared to enter yet another stressful situation—as Daddy would say.

It occurred to me that if this was their second year, and all this was going on, why on earth had they returned for still another summer? I asked them about it and they both replied that it was the best camp in the world.

"Besides the almost total lack of rules and supervision, where else can you find a camp with a brand-new candy store?" Lily said logically.

"A candy store!" I thought of all my gummy bears melting together under my bunk. "There's a candy store?"

"With video games and pizza to go. But I don't recommend the pizza unless you're absolutely desperate," Jen cautioned.

Mr. Hildebrande had come to the decision that since the kids were walking off the grounds to buy food and treats at the small country store down the road, they might as well buy it from the commissary instead. I supposed there was some logic in that.

We got to the stable, and they went cheerily towards their stalls while I wondered if my knees were going to buckle under me right then and there. Maybe they were exaggerating, I hoped. Maybe this was just some kind of friendly scare-treatment they gave to new girls, I thought. Maybe they were telling the truth, I feared, and went looking for the barn manager. If anyone could tell me what was going on, she could.

Barn managers are always such self-reliant, in-control-type people. I think it's from years of handling horses under all kinds of conditions. Nothing ever seems to upset or rattle or even rush them. When you're talking to a barn manager, you have to be prepared to take your time.

I went into the building through the rear doors and

followed the signs pointing to the stable office. It was kind of dark as I made my way past several empty stalls. The familiar aroma of leather and horses mixed with the sweet scent of hay; for me, this is what I imagine heaven must smell like.

"Hello," I called quietly as I slowly walked down the center aisle until my eyes became accustomed to the light.

"*Help!*" a voice screamed back.

"Hellooo," I said a little more loudly as things began to come into focus.

"*Helppp!*" the voice called again.

I looked in the direction of the sound. It was coming from just around the corner of the last stall. I ran the last few steps. It was Billie, the barn manager. She was leaning all her considerable weight against her office door, holding it closed.

"Hurry!" she said urgently. "Get that board and bring it over here." She puffed and sweated. "Help me prop it against the door!"

I looked at her and took a step backwards. Maybe she had cornered the county lunatic—I just hoped it wasn't poor Daddy again.

"Who's inside?" I asked quickly. If by some chance it was my father, I wasn't going to help board him in, and I really didn't want to be there if he broke out. Just the embarrassment would be enough to turn me to stone on the spot. "What's going on?"

"It's Demon!" she shouted. "He's taken over my office!"

"What happened?" I asked her.

"I'm not sure," she answered. "We had a buyer lined up for him, and I was filling out his sales papers when he galloped in and stepped on my typewriter."

Just then there was a loud whinny and a kick at the door that moved Billie two feet off-center.

"Hurry with that board!" she shouted, struggling to push the door shut again.

"Why don't you just let him out of there?" I asked her as I dragged the long plank of wood towards her straining body.

"What?" she asked.

"Why don't you just let him out of the office? You know, maybe he's through typing and he wants to go home now. Let's just open the door and stand back."

"Say," she said enthusiastically, "that's a thought. I don't know all that much about horses," she explained.

"Aren't you the barn manager?"

"Yes," she explained. "But just until they rebuild the swimming pool. I'm really a lifeguard. Now stand back, or better yet, stand in one of the closed stalls, or be prepared to run for your life. I'm letting go."

She pulled the door open and stood hidden behind it. Just as I thought, Demon was happy to be leaving the office for the day. He ran down the aisle, out of the barn, and into the far meadow, where he settled down to spend the summer in the rough. Certainly no one at the camp was going to try to capture him.

After Demon trotted happily out of the barn, Billie looked relieved and wiped the sweat from her brow. "Things like that never happen around a swimming pool," she said, and looked at her office, newly decorated by Demon. "I sure hope they rebuild it soon." Then she sat down heavily on the floor and began to breathe deeply in an effort to relax. I wondered if she was a psychologist as well as a lifeguard.

I asked her why she didn't do her lifeguarding down at the lake.

"The lake?" she asked, shuddering. Then she looked from side to side as if to make sure we were alone. "You don't ever want to go swimming in that lake," she confided. "You don't ever even want to fall in." She winked a huge, confidential wink at me, and I felt a chilly shudder run up and down my back.

"Is there," I asked her quietly, fully prepared to let my imagination run away with me in a spooky cause, "something dangerous in the lake?"

"Yes," she said. "But we don't like to talk about it."

"A monster? A shark? Something too awful to mention?" I could feel the surface of my skin forming little hills and gullies like the surface of an old-fashioned washboard.

"Garbage," she said.

"Garbage? Euchh."

"You said it," she said. "It comes from the boys' camp on the other side. They throw it in because they know the wind will carry it in our direction. You know how boys are," she said, and we both agreed that yes, indeed, we both knew how boys were.

Billie asked me what I wanted, and I told her that I was a day late.

"In that case," she said as she got up, "let's see about getting you a horse. Wait here; I'll get my list." She went into the office and came out with a clipboard, which she studied carefully. "It looks like," she said, checking the list again, "it comes down to a choice of two. And," she added, "if you take my advice, it comes down to a choice of one."

If there's one thing I like, it's being able to make my own choices. Billie led me past Solitaire's stall, and he looked out at us with his ears plastered straight back and down on his head. In case you don't know much about horses, ears plastered straight back and down is not a good sign.

"You don't want to ride him," Billie cautioned as if she were letting me in on a big secret.

"You're right," I agreed. Then she motioned me towards the last stall in the place. And there was Blue.

"Wait here," she said. "I'll bring him out." She opened the gate and called, "Here, horsey horsey. Come on now."

I'm not sure who thought it was more strange, me or Blue, but he came out and nuzzled me gently. I led him outside so that I could at least see him more clearly in the daylight. He was beautiful. A large dapple gray that in the sunlight looked blue. I could see where he got his name. Why, I wondered, had Lily and Jen carried on so about him?

Billie followed me out of the barn holding a saddle.

"Do you know how to put one of these things on?" she asked. I said I did and she handed it to me and watched me intently as I lifted it onto Blue's back. I asked Billie if there was anything she could tell me about Blue before I mounted. She said he was a sweetheart of a horse. Then she added, in a quick, matter-of-fact way that made me wonder, "Oh yes, Blue's former owner had taught him some tricks. But nothing dangerous," she added quickly.

"I'm glad to hear that," I said, tightening the girth and adjusting the stirrups. Then I swung into the saddle. "What kind of tricks?" I asked her, evening out my reins.

"Just tricks," she said. "Nothing to worry about."

As far as I was concerned, I was happy just to be on a horse in the sunshine.

"Ride him around to get used to him," Billie suggested. "Take him out to the field."

Carefully, I turned Blue's head in the right direction and very gently touched my heel to his side. "Walk!" I said firmly, and Blue sat down on his rump.

Chapter Eight

I don't know if you've ever had a horse sit down
while you were on its back. Or if you've ever had a
horse that sat down at all. I certainly never had. I'd
never even seen it done before. I've been on horses
that have rolled over, fallen over, tripped over, and
even jumped over. But Blue was the first to ever just
plain sit down. What could he be thinking, I wondered
once I decided that the world wasn't coming to an end.

To say that I was surprised doesn't begin to describe
my feelings. For a minute I imagined I knew what it
must be like to get caught in an earthquake and have
the ground just open up under you. Even shocked is
not the word that could adequately tell you how it felt
as Blue settled himself comfortably on his haunches
like someone about to read the morning paper.

Naturally, the first and fastest thing I did was to
obey the law of gravity. I slid out of the saddle backwards and down his back until we were both seated on

his rump. To be more exact, Blue was on his rump, I was on his tail, and his tail was on the ground.

"That's one of the tricks I told you about," Billie said helpfully. She didn't seem very concerned. In fact, she chuckled a bit.

"I kind of guessed that already," I said. "Tell me something, Billie. Do I look as ridiculous as I feel?"

"That depends on just how ridiculous you feel," she said, helping me out of my stirrups and to my feet.

Blue just sat there, looking at me with an expression on his face that I can only describe as satisfied. His ears were nice and forward and happy-looking. He looked like he expected some small reward for his efforts. He seemed to think there was at least a carrot lurking in his future. In a way, I could see his point. After all, he was only doing what his former owner had trained him to do, and he did it well, too. At least I think he did it well. I had no previous experience with sitting horses to compare him with.

"Here," said Billie, taking a lump of sugar from her pocket and handing it to me. "If you don't give him something, he'll never get up."

I unwrapped the sugar, and the familiar sound of the paper tearing caused Blue's eyes to widen in happy expectation. Personally, I had qualms about offering Blue a reward for doing something I didn't want him to do just so he would do something I did want him to do, namely, stand up.

I hesitated for a minute or two while I wondered what Daddy would have to say about that. He'd probably say that I was reinforcing negative behavior. He'd say that bribery never worked and that giving in to this form of blackmail was not a solution. He'd say that the only thing that could possibly solve the problem was deep and long-term analysis.

Then he'd schedule an appointment for Blue to see him at his office four times a week at least. But then again, my father doesn't ride horses, so he wouldn't care if Blue sat in his office all day. I think he charges by the hour.

I decided to reanalyze the situation. This time from the judicial point of view, the way my mother would if she were in my place.

Legally, Blue was supposed to let me ride him around. It was in the camp contract. Anyway, at least I think it was in the contract. Anyway, I was sure it was in the brochure. I did remember that it did say each camper would have her own horse to love and care for all summer. I tried to remember whether it said anything about each camper riding the horse that she loved and cared for all summer. Did it say anything? Or did I just take it for granted? I might have gotten stuck with a giant house pet to love and care for all summer. How do these things happen? And why do they happen to me?

I made a mental list of all the pros and cons, and the ethics of bribery, as I held the sugar cube until it began to get sticky against the palm of my hand. I admit that the cons, both legal and scientific, far outweighed the pros, so I came to the only decision that decency allowed. I gave him the sugar, and he popped up on all fours like a jack-in-the-box. There were some guilt feelings about caving in to pressure like that, but after all, I hadn't come to camp to teach morality to a horse.

I climbed back into the saddle while Billie gave me some pointers as to how Blue operated.

"First of all," she said, handing me the reins, "if you want him to go forward, you say *whoa.*"

Now whoa is something I'd never said to a horse,

with the exception of the time I was three years old and my parents took me for a hansom-cab ride around Central Park.

"What," I asked in my best sarcastic tone of voice, "do you say to stop him—*giddyap?*"

"Whatever you do," Billie warned, "don't say giddyap. It gives him the hiccups." And sure enough, a mighty hiccup emerged from Blue. "Here," she said, handing me another lump of sugar, "it's the only thing that brings him around."

Blue turned his head towards me at the sound of the paper tearing again and hiccuped.

Billie needn't have worried about my saying giddyap, because the last time I ever said that to a horse was on the same buggy ride that I said whoa.

"Now go ahead," Billie encouraged me. "Show him who's boss. And here," she added, reaching into her pocket and handing me several cubes of sugar, "you may need these."

I tried to slip them into my pocket unnoticed, but Blue's big eyes watched every move. I got the impression he already had a pretty good idea who was boss. He was. But I made up my mind right then and there to mold him into the best hunter-jumper the camp had ever seen.

Now all that was left was to make up his mind about it.

"Whoa," I said firmly and nudged his side with my heel. Blue turned his head, looked at my foot, and then bit me on my toes.

"Don't kick him," Billie advised. "He doesn't like it."

"Is there anything else I should know?" I asked her, counting the tooth marks on my boot.

Billie said she couldn't think of anything right off-hand, then added that once Blue and I got to know each other, we'd make a fine pair. I was glad to hear that at least, and hoped that I lived long enough for us to get to know each other in the first place. Then she asked if I could swim, and I said I could. She said that swimming him in the lake was good for the occasional lameness she'd forgotten to mention.

"Whoa!" I said to him again, and slowly, one foot in front of the other, off he went in the direction of the training ring next to the road. But then he headed straight for the lake.

My father's car was parked nearby, with my mother behind the wheel and Daddy curled up in the rear seat, snoring happily. There was already a rumor going around that he suffered from sleeping sickness, and some campers claimed that it was catching.

When Mama saw us coming, she got out and admired my horse. She said that Blue and I made a fine pair. Knowing what I knew about Blue, I wondered what she meant by that.

"I'm driving your father back to the city," my mother said as she smiled at me and my mount. "I'll be back on Friday afternoon or Saturday morning. I want to clear up some work at my office so I can take some time off to spend with my kids," she said, smiling bravely at our parting.

Then she got into the car as fast as she could, waved once again, and drove off down the road in the direction of the city and home. I had a few pangs of despair as I watched her go, and I wished that Daddy had woken up long enough to say good-bye. But Mama said that letting him sleep was an act of pure charity. At least I had Blue, and we went for a swim—in the garbage-strewn lake.

It took a few days for camp to settle down into a familiar routine: Serena's surprise attacks, visits to the candy store, mucking out the stables, gathering food for Joan, who never wanted to get out of bed except to go to the bathroom.

Some people said that whatever it was that my father had, Joan seemed to have caught it. Lily said it wasn't true, because Joan was asleep in her bunk long before my father even showed up. Joan admitted that was true, and I was relieved. The last thing I needed was a burden of guilt over her condition. It's not as if she stayed asleep all the time, though. She was wide-awake during prime-time television hours, and sometimes she wandered around the fields gathering inspiration for an epic poem she was writing to her boyfriend back home.

She particularly liked rhyming things with moon, and loon, and June, and tune, and spent a good deal of time working spoon and croon into her verse. At night, during commercials and station breaks, she'd read us her day's efforts. The rest of us agreed that basically boys weren't worth all the effort she was going through. Not yet anyway, and not ever, when there were horses around.

We did a lot of talking about parents splitting up. Jen said she was an authority on the subject as her parents had been married three times each.

"My birthdays are like Christmas," she added happily. "I get presents from six different people. And that doesn't even include my three stepbrothers and two half-sisters."

Jen advised us to stay on good terms with stepparents past and present, as they were an excellent source of gifts and money, which balanced out the unwanted advice.

Lily said her parents were still very much together but communicated with each other mainly through their telephone-answering machine. Her mother had a career and played tennis, and her father had an office and a sailboat, so they didn't have too much spare time on their hands. In her house, the blinking message light meant that someone wasn't coming home for dinner.

Joan was of the opinion that we were all lucky, because, as far as she could tell, her parents were never married in the first place.

"They get along too well for that. It's positively unnatural. They never even disagree with each other," she said. Then she went back to sleep, right in the middle of one of her favorite programs, so we got a chance to change the channel.

I told them about my mother and father, and Albert, and Fluff. Jen thought that Fluff was the name of my father's girlfriend and said it sounded like the name of a chorus girl. Then she said that from the sound of the arrangements, it didn't sound to her as if my mother and Albert were involved. "He might be a red herring," she said.

"A what?" Joan asked.

"A red herring," Jen explained. "You know, something to take your attention away from the real fly-in-the-ointment."

Then she asked me if there were any men in my mother's life whom she didn't talk about.

"If she doesn't talk about them," I said, "how can I possibly know?"

"There," Jen said, as if she'd proven something very profound, "what did I tell you?"

There was no way for me to tell what she'd told me. I looked at Lily to see if she could tell me what Jen had told me, but she just shrugged her shoulders in a kind of noncommittal way. There was just no ignoring

Jen's advice in matters like these. She, after all, had a lot more experience than I did. In fact, with several different sets of parents, she had more experience than the rest of us put together. Maybe there was someone other than Albert. Maybe he was a pink salmon, or whatever she'd called him. I made up my mind to be on the alert. The weekends would tell.

In the meantime, I spent my days trying to transform Blue into the winning competitor I knew he could be. The problem seemed to be convincing him. At least I knew that if we ever entered a sugar-cube-eating contest, we'd take first prize. But there was something very lovable about Blue. And, in his own way, he was very smart. He could paw the ground four times if you asked him how much two plus two was and nod his head vigorously if you asked him if he was a horse. However, when it came to going through our paces in the training ring, he preferred to stand and watch from the sidelines, with one front leg crossed casually over the other.

Once in a while, Serena, who, in addition to the marvelous job she was doing as our counselor, was our riding instructor, would show up and give us the benefit of her experience and wisdom. She was a great help. When she wasn't training her own horse, she offered the rest of us all kinds of constructive encouragement.

"Move that horse, lard butt," she'd shout. "What do you need, a steering wheel?"

If she was really feeling perky, she'd help get your horse in motion by running after both of you with her riding crop. We all admitted that at least she took our minds off our other problems. She even got Joan up and about by removing the springs from her bed while she was in the bathroom. Joan came out, plunked onto her mattress, and went straight through to the floor with it.

All in all, we didn't have much time to be homesick, but I confess that for the first few days I was. I wondered how Wil was doing across the lake, playing soccer and floating garbage toward our shore.

I found myself looking forward to the weekend and the sight of our car coming down the road, so I could ask Mama if there was anyone she didn't want me to ask her about. I was also looking forward to dinner off camp, if you could call her house across the road off camp. Jen, Lily, and even Joan asked to be invited.

"When any of my sets of parents show up," Jen promised, "you can come with us to dinner."

"Mine, too!" Joan and Lily quickly agreed.

What all of us really needed was a good meal. It had been a week by then, and it was almost impossible to look another slice of Hildebrande's pizza in the eye.

Chapter Nine

Mama took to arriving earlier and earlier every Friday. Daddy couldn't stand that. She also took to renting cars instead of driving up with him or Albert. Daddy couldn't stand that either.

He said that there was nothing worse than someone who neglected her work at the office. Mama just pointed to the bulging briefcase that accompanied her everywhere she went except to the bathroom.

She was lucky. She could bring work from her office, sit on the screened front porch of the summer house, and even take Mondays off if she wished.

My father said he was surprised at her for taking unfair advantage of the fact that it was impossible for him to leave his office early at the end of the week.

"Fridays are very important to my patients," he explained when I asked him. "They don't like to feel that they're going off to face the weekend alone."

Mama said that the only reson Fridays were so important to my father and his patients was that a lot of them got paid on Fridays and it was a good time to hand them their bills.

Daddy got very annoyed at that. Maybe annoyed isn't exactly the right word. I think he would use the word defensive, if he were talking about someone else —like Mama, for instance. Daddy got very defensive at that.

He seemed to think that Mama was questioning his professional ethics, but Mama said that was the last thing in the world she'd ever even think of doing.

"If there's one thing I know, at least," she said, "it's that you're a good psychologist and you've helped many people set their lives in order."

I couldn't believe it! For the first time in ages, Mama was saying something nice about Daddy. He couldn't believe it either and mumbled something about her being a capable lawyer. He didn't say it too enthusiastically though, or at least not enthusiastically enough for my mother, because she said it was a wonder that, considering how able an analyst he was, he still wasn't able to straighten out some of his own quirks. And she said the word *quirks* as if it were spelled in capital letters.

It was Daddy's turn to get all stiff this time. "Quirks?" he said. "Quirks? I do not have quirks!"

I sat back and relaxed. They were sounding more like the folks I knew and loved. At least it fit right in with their behavior over the last several months.

I'd made up my mind that it was entirely up to them whether or not they stayed together. If staying together would make them happy, fine. If splitting up would make them happy, fine. There really wasn't much I could do about it one way or the other, so the best thing I could do was to be philosophical about it.

But I did want them to be consistent. What was supposed to happen to my need for equilibrium?

Mama smiled when Daddy said he had no quirks. As a lawyer, she thinks everybody has them. As long as they're legal, she really doesn't mind.

"You do so have quirks," she said very cool and quite matter-of-factly, except for the word *quirks*. She said that again with a lot of emphasis, and this time Daddy got out-and-out angry, not defensive. He said that Mama was talking about something else entirely.

Mama just laughed and asked what. I prepared myself for some juicy secrets I'd never known before. My father's quirks. If they were going to start having arguments that revealed all sorts of new knowledge, I was perfectly prepared to listen. Usually, when they had a serious discussion, they made sure Wil and I were overhearing it safely from inside our rooms. But here it was, a short, hot summer, and they were letting it all hang out. Luckily, I had several gummy bears in my pocket, and I popped them into my mouth before my mother noticed and complained about how I was ruining my braces.

Daddy said that what he had was discipline. And then he patted his checkbook pocket. I don't know why he patted his checkbook pocket, except that maybe discipline is cheaper than quirks.

He said there was nothing worse than someone who spent a lot of money. "Nothing worse," he repeated, very quietly, for emphasis. "In other words, a spendthrift."

Mama said there was one thing worse, and that was someone, she said even more quietly, for emphasis, who never spent any money. "In other words, a cheapskate."

After all that tempting talk about quirks, things

were back to normal in our household. My mother and my father were arguing about money. Summer home, sweet summer home.

At least it wasn't a complete loss. As in the past, when that particular debate came up, I got ten dollars. Wil would have gotten ten dollars, too, had he been around, but his camp was farther away, the food was edible, and he was apparently enjoying his summer playing soccer. It was too much to expect him to attend the family bouts. It was easier for me. I could just walk across the road, have a sandwich, watch the show, and get paid for it besides.

Mama went to her purse and whipped out a five-dollar bill. Then she handed it to me to show Daddy that she could spend her money any way she wanted to, and whenever she wanted to, and on whatever, for whomever.

"This is for you," she said as usual, handing the bill to me. Then, after Daddy groaned, he creaked open his wallet and gave me five soft old singles to show Mama that he could be just as generous as she could be anytime he wanted.

"Buy something useful," he said, trying to look brave about parting with money, even though I knew that nothing in the whole wide world causes him more pain.

I listened to them for a while, hoping they might admit something dreadful that we could all gasp and feel awful about. Some shameful scandal that would explain why Daddy was sleeping in a bag up a tree. Some unforgivable piece of treachery done by one to the other. Something so grossly, overwhelmingly despicable on somebody's part that only the love I bore the guilty party could help me overlook, and forgive, and not quite forget.

Instead, as usual, they went directly from their number-one favorite argument about money to their number-two fallback: who had proposed to whom. It seemed very important to them, Daddy in particular. You would think there was some kind of prize for the correct answer.

I personally didn't care who had proposed to whom. Not even the first time they trotted that one out. I wanted to hear why they were breaking up. I wanted to hear something horrid I could sink my understanding into. Maybe a tidbit I could quietly cry myself to sleep over for a few nights. Something delicious.

I waited, and very patiently too, but they went straight into their who-was-spoiling-the-children-rotten number, and they both looked at me. I decided to take that personally, so I got up and announced that I was going back to camp, and I left them arguing happily.

Naturally, when I went back to my bunk, I took the opportunity to discuss my situation with someone who'd gone through it many times before. Jen was of the opinion that my parents were still going through the premassive guilt stage of our parent, child, and family relationship. She was right, I thought. They'd certainly looked guilty about it when I marched out the door.

"They're still only separated," Jen observed after giving it a lot of thought. "I've seen it before. Five dollars here, five dollars there," she said, snapping her fingers as if the amount were too trivial to think about. "Just wait till they get a divorce and the thoughts of how badly they've failed their offspring begin to eat away at their brains," she added enthusiastically. "Then make up a shopping list. It's present time all day long."

I asked her how long each stage lasted. Jen said it all depended.

"For instance," she explained, "in my case, my mother, the first time around anyway, was a regular cornucopia in the clothing department. It got embarrassing. I was outgrowing clothes I never even had a chance to wear.

"This," Jen explained, "was after the strictly cold-cash stage, when she thought that selecting my wardrobe would prove that she loved me. It seemed very important to her. I preferred the cash, but it's so hard to discuss those things with your parents."

Jen said that her father went through his stages much more slowly, so it took him a little while to catch up to the changes.

"He travels a lot," Jen explained. "He used that as an excuse to send me checks from all over the world. I loved that. But then everything changed when my mother got engaged to be married for the second time.

"She accused my father of trying to buy my affection, and I was all in favor of it. I guess it kind of got to him though, and that's when my father decided I needed ice-skating equipment. I like ice-skating, but my room began to look like a skate shop. I even had a hockey stick! What was I supposed to do with that? Besides, my ankles absolutely kill me when I try to ice-skate more than once a week. Finally I got him to get me interested in collecting coins and foreign currency. At least they'll be worth something someday."

"What did your mother do?" I asked her. "Did she go on buying you clothes?"

"Yes," Jen said, sighing. "But the styles got younger and younger the closer it got to the day of her wedding. Finally she started buying me striped overalls

80

with bunnies on them. Where she got them in my size, I'll never know. I think she had them custom-made.

"I expected a box of diapers to show up on my bureau any second. I don't think she wanted to trot down the aisle with an almost-teenager cheering her on from the sidelines. She wanted to be young and in love, and who was I to stand in her way?

"Then," Jen said and laughed, "she asked me to be her flower girl! That was a charming experience. She bought me a baby-pink-and-blue organdy extravaganza with lots of bows, about two sizes too short. I looked precious. But instead of looking younger for her new in-laws, I looked slightly retarded, and they began to wonder what their darling son had gotten himself into."

"How did she act after she remarried?" I asked, as this was something I really wanted to know. Was my mother going to stuff me into a pinafore for Albert's sake? How about Daddy? Could I expect a jungle gym on my doorstep?

"Well," Jen said, getting up from her bunk to stretch, "her clothes urge kind of evened out with the last of the closet space. It was loaded with things I wouldn't wear. And you have to remember, as a blushing bride she didn't have all that much time to think about guilt."

"You mean she stopped feeling guilty?" I was shocked. Did Mama intend to stop handing out the fives?

"Yes, I think so," said Jen, trying to recall the details. "It seems to me that after the wedding she went straight from feeling guilty to ignoring me completely."

"You mean, just because she got remarried, she ignored you!" I was feeling a little shaken. Would Mama ever ignore me? Could such a thing happen?

"I hear new love does that to people," Jen said, and we both shrugged our shoulders at the mysteries of parents.

"I'm not complaining," she added quickly. "My new stepfather wanted me to like him, so he took up the slack. They always do that. He even bought me tickets to the circus, if you can believe that. I mean, seriously, I was already almost twelve years old and he wanted to send me and a friend to the circus! But what can you expect, the way my mother was dressing me? But he did at least try, so I more or less liked him."

That's when I decided that Albert couldn't be a candidate for stepfatherhood. He'd never even bought me so much as a pencil. In fact, he took the attitude that he was my mother's friend and lawyer and didn't seem to care whether I liked him or not.

That attitude, and his devotion to Fluff, were the only two things I liked about him. It just so happened that I didn't care whether or not he liked me. At least we had something in common, and it made life easier. I know he didn't like my ordering Shirley Temples in restaurants instead of straight ginger ale. That's where our attitudes came in handy. As I didn't care whether or not he liked me, I didn't have to care what he did or didn't like me doing.

What I wanted to know more about from Jen was this being-ignored-by-her-mother part of the arrangement. "How long did it last?" I asked her.

"Oh, not long," Jen said and reassured me. "Just about right up to and until her second divorce. Wow, you should have seen her then. She immediately started to feel guilty again. Even my ex-stepfather felt guilty and started sending me coins for my collection—some pretty good ones, too.

"My mother and I started taking ballet classes together, and when my ankles hurt, she'd discuss my schoolwork and social life. It began to get a little sticky. I mean, my feet were killing me and I wanted her to be my mother, not my girlfriend. I thought she was going to want to double-date any minute. Two more months of ballet and I'd have had to ride horses in a wheelchair. But then she got engaged again and stopped speaking to me altogether—until the wedding plans fell through. After that happened, it was seven months before she met and married my number-two stepfather in a whirlwind courtship."

"Was it a long seven months?" I asked her.

"She went into her buddies routine again. Only this time, she moved her bed into my room."

Chapter Ten

The summer went by with one lovely day blending into another. I spent a good deal of my time at the stable, talking over my problems with Blue. You may not believe it, but horses understand almost everything you tell them. Blue was very patient and nice about my problems and an excellent listener besides. His wide, consoling eyes made me feel better as I told him my troubles. If what Jen said about her parents applied to mine, things were going to get much worse in my world before they at least improved to bad.

Blue was a sweetheart of concern. He'd sit in one corner of his stall munching a carrot and nodding his head a lot, particularly if there were flies around. He looked very wise, though most of the time I wasn't sure he agreed with what I was saying. But I didn't mind. Blue was always a sympathetic listener, and I could tell him anything. That alone was a comfort.

I could tell Jen anything too, but then she'd always

tell me how whatever I was telling her reminded her of a particular situation she'd gone through. Then she'd tell me something more awful about her experiences. I know she was just trying to make me feel more hopeful about things, but somehow I always felt just the opposite.

I'd more or less been ready for my folks' marriage falling apart. It really didn't bother me as much as I thought it might or should. It was the thought of all those stepparents waltzing in and out of my life that I was worried about. It seemed to me that our apartment was small enough already without having to think about taking a series of strangers through. Jen asked me what Albert's living accommodations were like. I had to admit I didn't know. The only time I saw Albert was when he was at our house. For all I knew, he could be living in the street between visits. Jen said that was a bad sign—it might mean he wanted to move in with us. She was only trying to help, and I know they say that misery loves company, but sometimes my misery felt better when I shared it with my horse.

I asked Mama what Albert's apartment was like, specifically how many rooms. She didn't have the slightest idea either. Jen might be right. Albert might be after our real estate! That's a very serious problem in the city, what with the shortage of apartments and outrageous rents.

As for my parents, their argument now seemed to focus on which of them had never taken his or her rightful turn looking for a parking space for the car—that was Daddy's favorite accusation. And who shirked putting the garbage into the hall Tuesday, Thursday, and Saturday nights when the janitor made his rounds—Mama's pet peeve.

The only time Mama and Daddy seemed to stop feuding was on Saturday nights when practically half the camp showed up at my mother's house for a barbecue on the lawn. On those occasions, they appeared to get along the way they used to. They argued, of course, but at least it wasn't home-wrecking. It was also the only time there was decent food available to most of us.

Albert quickly became everybody's favorite cook and was quite masterful at charbroiling spareribs, which he soaked overnight in secret ingredients. Our camp nurse, Miss Maxwell, was becoming very fond of Albert, and I think that he was becoming fond of her. I began to feel sorry for my mother. Here she was losing a husband and a boyfriend all at the same time. But if she cared, she didn't show it, and I began to realize that she really didn't care. So I started to like Albert a little more, and he always saved me the ribs with the most meat on them.

At first, Daddy said that the situation between Albert and his new friend was disgraceful, and he said it a lot to Mama. Then he'd mutter something about her choice of friends and tenants and point to that as further evidence that, as far as men were concerned, she was still a babe in the woods.

Whenever he said that, Mama would take a step back, nod her head in agreement, and say that he was right, because look at whom she'd married. I could tell that secretly Daddy was pleased at Albert's new prospects. He and Albert even started to get along behind the big buffet table they made out of two barrels and some long boards. Daddy was in charge of the potato salad, which he made all by himself. Jen told me that she'd come to the conclusion that he was really very nice and not the cad she thought he was at first. And, she added, she was very fond of his potato salad. I was glad to hear that. Who needs your bunkmate thinking that your father is a cad who serves lousy potato salad?

Even Mr. Hildebrande started to attend our Saturday evening soirees. Mama put him in charge of the lemonade, and he made the rounds, making sure no guests dripped barbecue sauce onto their camp T-shirts.

I began to wonder whether there was a chance of a reconciliation in our household, and one or two Sundays, I even saw my parents talking to each other as if they were human beings. It was, after all, summertime, and there's always something romantic about that. I began to feel a little less nervous about the prospects of breaking in a whole new set of assorted family members.

Mama took the entire last two and a half weeks of the summer off, and Daddy began arriving on Wednesday evenings. Things were looking positive on the home front, and I spent more and more of my time preparing for the big horse show. Blue was really coming along nicely, and for the sake of his teeth, I began to cut apples into cube-size chunks, wrapping them in paper that made a satisfying tearing noise. Then Mama announced that her mother was coming up to camp to see me ride, and Daddy started to sulk again. He started going for long walks in the woods by himself and would come back covered with mosquito bites. It seems that the musk oil Mr. Hildebrande sold him at the beginning of the summer worked best at repelling human beings. Poor Daddy reeked of it and began to smell like an ox in season. I didn't mind. He was, after all, my father, and as long as he washed his hands before handling the potatoes, there didn't seem to be any harm in it.

I don't know why the thought of Grandma's visit upset him so much. But then again it always did. Personally, I was looking forward to Grandma seeing me ride. She'd been an excellent horsewoman when she was younger, and I wanted to show her what I could do. Needless to say, she and Daddy never quite hit it off. Once she told my mother that had she known her only daughter would marry such a weirdo, she'd have remained childless. I always thought that, secretly, way down deep inside, they really liked each other. But it was so secret, and so deep, that even they didn't know it. Things can sometimes happen that way. I'm totally sure of it.

The week leading up to the weekend of the horse show was a very exciting one. Everybody ran around getting herself and her horse groomed and ready. Even Joan got out of bed, although, as it turned out, she just wanted to wash her sheets. Lily sprained her wrist polishing her saddle, and Jen's boots gave her a blister on one of her heels. The glory of our cabin was resting on Blue's shoulders and mine.

I took Blue out to the course when no one was around, and we went through it together beautifully. I explained very carefully and several times to him how the Saturday show was to be the big event of the season and attended by camps for miles around. I didn't mention that the next day we were going to be visited by Wil's camp from across the lake. I wasn't sure how Blue felt about boys, but I did know that some horses absolutely loathe them.

Between the tension of preparing to show and the tension of an impending invasion by a herd of boys, I didn't have much time to think about anybody's troubles but my own. Even my parents and Albert had their hands full. Since it was such a special occasion, they were going to have their Saturday night barbecue on Sunday evening, for the boys as well as their regular guests. Every time I saw my father, he was peeling a potato.

Before I knew it, the big show morning arrived—and my grandmother along with it. I could have used another week just to get ready, and I know that Daddy felt the same way, except in his case he was thinking in terms of years.

The day was beautiful. There was a little chilly nip in the air, as if fall and school were waiting their turn nearby. It was good riding weather though. The horses would be more frisky and not get overheated so easily. Even Fluff was feeling her oats and barked at everybody until Albert locked her in the cottage.

Then I saw my grandmother's 1948 Packard limousine coming down the road. It's a real antique and looked almost as big as the camp's barn. It was being driven, as usual, by Old Tim, the driver who's been with her family since before my mother was born. He'd worked for my grandfather and is even older than Grandma, if that's possible. We all have to show Old Tim a lot of consideration, or Grandma gets annoyed and threatens to cut us out of her will. Nobody in my family seems to want that, especially Mama.

She even told Albert to save Old Tim my meaty spareribs, because I think he has gums where his teeth used to be. I pointed out that those meaty spareribs she was being so free with were mine by a long summer tradition and one of the few things I thought I could count on. Mama soothed me quietly and said I should try to understand. When I asked her what I should try to understand, she said that I should try to understand that she wanted to inherit Grandma's money. That I could understand.

It took about fifteen minutes from the time I first saw the car just a few hundred yards away until Old Tim pulled into the parking lot and drove right through it, past the grandstand, across the grass, and finally stopped near the stadium jumping course next to the seats so Grandma wouldn't have to walk far. Her legs sometimes ache, and she leans lightly on an elegant black walking stick with a carved ivory handle that used to belong to my grandfather.

The car came to a halt by the first row, where Daddy had staked out the three best seats bright and early at my mother's request so that Grandma, Mama, and he wouldn't miss anything. He hadn't tried to save Albert a seat, because Albert was spending the morning marinating his famous spareribs in his secret sauce and said that horses made him itch.

Daddy was dozing when the car pulled up, and it took Old Tim five minutes just to turn off the engine. He drives very, very slowly, and I wondered if it had taken them as long to get up to camp as it had us. He spent the next five minutes trying to get his door open so that he could get out and open the rear door for my grandmother. But she was out before he was and opened his door for him, because Old Tim needs assistance getting in and out of the car.

I was already mounted on Blue, and I waved to Grandma and she waved back, and I was really happy to see her whether she remembers me in her will or not.

Grandma helped Old Tim out from behind the wheel, and he took off his chauffeur's cap, waved to me with it, and almost lost his balance. Then she and Mama helped him towards the seats where Daddy sat napping happily. Grandma counted the available chairs and then tapped Daddy lightly on the head with her cane until he was startled into waking up and helping Old Tim into his former seat. Daddy was a good sport about it and always very polite to Grandma. I don't think he wanted us to be cut out of her will either. Grandma, on the other hand, always looked at Daddy as if he were contagious.

Mama smiled and acted bright and happy. Even Daddy smiled and acted bright and happy. She was jolly, and he was jolly. He fetched Grandma's lap robe from the trunk of the car, and Mama smiled, and he smiled. She suggested that he draw up another chair all bright and happy and jolly and smiling, and he did so, all bright and happy and jolly and smiling.

I couldn't believe my eyes. Even Blue was shocked. When I looked at Mama with my what-the-heck-is-going-on look, she looked back at me with her cool-it-or-else look.

Grandma may not have been overjoyed at the fact that Daddy was her son-in-law, but from what I knew about her, she liked separations and divorces even less. My parents didn't seem anxious to tell her the good news. I think in a way they were both just a little bit afraid of this frail but formidable old lady and her large and formidable estate.

After a few minutes of all the bright, happy, jolly smiles, I noticed Grandma looking at Mama with her what-the-heck-is-going-on look. Mama noticed it too and looked at Daddy with her she-wants-to-know-what's-going-on look. Daddy looked at Grandma, and she looked at him, and he looked at Mama. Then the two of them made an effort to calm down from being so jolly and began to behave very correctly towards each other. They were so correct that they could hardly move without creaking.

Then Grandma, who's a wise old bird, looked at me, and I looked at her, and I wondered if she was going to leave all her money to the trees.

I tried to change the atmosphere by asking her what she thought of my horse, and she asked me if a milk wagon came with it. Then we both laughed gaily, as if we thought she was joking. Then Mama and Daddy laughed, as if they thought she was joking, but they laughed a little too long, and everybody looked at everybody. Of all the laughing and joking people there, only Old Tim was enjoying himself. He sat in Daddy's chair and was fast asleep in no time.

Mr. Hildebrande stopped by and said hello, and then he went to the center of the enclosure and attempted to blow several notes on his hunting horn to call the meet to order. He huffed and puffed and succeeded in sounding like an elephant burping, and the competition began.

One by one the riders rounded the jump course, and one by one they managed to rack up faults. Even Serena, the ace *numero uno* of the countryside, managed to knock over a rail on her last jump, and too soon it was my turn.

Blue and I went to the starting point, and I offered him tons of praise and encouragement. We'd done it all perfectly in many many practice sessions, and I tried not to tense up as we started. I decided that since everyone else had at least one penalty for either refusing jumps or knocking them down, all we had to do was get around the course without a mishap, and we'd win glory and ribbons. In a way I was feeling lucky. We had more than a good chance, as long as Blue didn't feel rushed. There was no need to rush, because no one had jumped a clean round, so there was no need to race against the clock.

We went perfectly. The only jump I was worried about was the next-to-the-last high fence. Blue approached it slowly and sailed right over with his legs tucked neatly to his stomach. I was thrilled. He went even slower as we neared the last jump. We were near victory, victory over the doubters and particularly over our counselor, whom we'd taken to calling Mad Serena after she tried to set the chef's hat on fire. What glory! I could see it all laid out in front of me. Camp Champ!

I didn't want to hurry, so I reined Blue in and we approached the jump at a little more than a crawl. Just as we neared it, Blue and I passed in front of my cheering family.

Daddy shouted, "Go for it!"

Mama called, "One more to go!" Grandma gave me a thumbs-up sign. Some of my friends came rushing to the rail and joined in the encouragement, and I thought my heart would burst right on the spot.

Jen yelled, "Come on Tin," and Joan waved parts of her clean laundry from our cabin door. Lily flapped her sprained wrist on the sidelines and urged me to score one for the Gipper, whoever that was, but she seemed to know and it seemed very important to her.

The ribbons, the cup, the honor of it all flashed in front of my eyes. It was thrilling. I didn't know whether to laugh or cry, but I forced myself to concentrate.

Even Albert caught the excitement. He came rushing over from across the road, itching and scratching and cheering me on. As Albert got closer to the horses, he let out an allergic sneeze that surprised Old Tim awake just in time for him to see me and Blue creeping slowly by before his sleepy eyes. Old Tim raised his cap in a dazed salute.

"Giddyap," he called out helpfully. *"Giddyap!"*

Well when Blue heard that, he immediately stood still and got the hiccups, and I began to bounce up and down in the saddle like a pogo stick. My whole cheering section stopped cheering and just looked at one another. They'd never seen anything quite like it.

"Don't stop now," Old Tim urged as he struggled to his feet. "Don't stop now. Walk on, you horse. *Walk on.*"

"Don't say that!" I yelled, reaching into my pocket and starting to peel apples squares as fast as I could.

"Don't say what?" almost everybody asked at once. "Don't say what?"

"Don't say *walk!*" I shouted, and Blue sat down.

Chapter Eleven

According to the rule books, each time a horse refuses a jump, five points are added to the rider's score as a penalty. The higher the score, the worse off you are. The question in our case seemed to be, just how badly off were we? Had Blue refused to take the jump—which was still twenty feet away—or was he just resting? I may have been just a little prejudiced in the matter, but it seemed to me that he was, after all, just resting. If anybody in the whole world agreed with me that that was the case, I'd just get a time penalty. That wouldn't be as bad as a refusal, depending on just how long my horse decided to sit around.

Luckily for us, the judges weren't sure either. In fact, I think they were just a little stunned. They scratched their heads, and then they put them together. They began to search the rules for some kind of precedent and conferred some more. I didn't just sit there while they were trying to figure it out. I got very busy trying to crawl up Blue's back and into the saddle. At least my feet were still in the stirrups, which made it more difficult, but I didn't want to be disqualified for dismounting.

The immediate problem I was facing was that every time I got halfway to my uphill goal, Blue would hiccup and send me sliding right back down again. It felt something like climbing a sand dune. The other problem I had was that Blue just wasn't interested in my pieces of apple. Oh, he ate them, all right. But he still wouldn't get up, especially not with me sitting on his tail.

Billie, the stable manager, suddenly appeared at our side and told me to remain calm. That was good news; at least Billie thought I was still calm. She had a real cube of sugar which she peeled as close to Blue's ear as she could while I clung to the back of my saddle. I had to hang on for dear life. Even if my faithful horse chose to do me a favor and get up on all fours, I'd still be perched on him someplace south of where I was supposed to be. I wondered if anybody in the history of the sport had ever ridden to glory from behind the saddle. It would be something like driving a racing car from the rear seat.

Blue heard the tearing noise of Billie's wrapper and perked up his ears. Then he very carefully inspected what was being offered him, just to make sure it wasn't another of my paper-covered pieces of apple. He sniffed, he snorted, and finally when he was satisfied that there was indeed a lump of sugar in his future, he chewed. Then he got up with me hanging on for dear life. It felt very undignified. Personally, I didn't care much how I looked—well, maybe I cared just a little bit—I just wanted to get over that last fence on his back somehow, hiccups and all.

Blue started off again before I was exactly ready. We bounced towards the barrier with my arms around his neck, and I'm happy to report that I did indeed go over the hurdle with several feet to spare. The only problem was that I went over the hurdle all by myself. I thought we were a team, but Blue had other things in mind as we neared the obstacle. He just stopped moving and I didn't, and he launched me on my first solo flight into space. Up, up I went, and suddenly I was flying. And even more suddenly, I was landing. I'd fallen off horses plenty of times before, but this was the first time one ever catapulted me off his back.

Grandma almost fainted, and the next thing I knew, she was shaking her walking stick in Mr. Hildebrande's face, demanding several explanations. He sputtered and stammered, and then offered to sell her the horse. Mama and Daddy, meanwhile, decided to take the opportunity to decide just whose fault it was I was up there at camp and on that horse in the first place. My whole cheering section had turned into a major riot. The only person who remained calm at all was Old Tim. He sat down, closed his eyes, and tried to doze off. Poor Albert was so shocked that he went into an extended sneezing fit and had to be helped back across the road by Nurse Maxwell, who, as it turned out, became ill whenever she saw people in pain.

Happily for me, I wasn't too hurt or at least not enough to show it. The last thing I needed was Nurse Maxwell getting sick all over me. My pride and feelings were crushed enough already—for that moment, anyway. I was, however, shocked at Blue's behavior. And after all the nice things I'd done for that horse, too! I'd fed him and washed him, brushed him and combed him. I even told him all my household problems, and this was the thanks I got. I mean, really, talk about ingratitude.

Jen leaped quickly over the fence to help me up. I got to my feet, swayed back and forth once or twice, and then brushed myself off to the cheers of the crowd. I looked over the jump at my ungrateful mount as angrily as I could. Blue looked back at me, and you know, I think he was smiling! Even his hiccups were gone.

Grandma called to me, and she reached through the rails to give me a hug, then she shook her cane at Mr. Hildebrande again. Mama and Daddy paused in their argument to take a breath, and they both noticed that Grandma was noticing them. They stopped battling immediately and asked me what had happened. It seemed perfectly clear to me what had happened. What else could they possibly want to know? What did they expect, an instant replay?

Needless to say, the judges had found what they were looking for, and Blue and I were eliminated. My counselor won the event. She was a good sport about it though, and after her victory ride around the field, she offered me her ribbon just for not breaking my neck. She said it would have looked bad for her. Imagine how it would have looked for me. I didn't accept the ribbon, of course. Then Serena said that I was all right in her book, and I decided that maybe she wasn't so bad after all. Blue walked daintily around the jump and nuzzled my back with his nose, so we forgave each other immediately, and I led him back to the barn. Then I fed him and washed him, brushed him and combed him, and he sat down in his stall and listened quietly while I told him my troubles all over again. This time they included losing the horse show of the season. When I was finished, I had a good, old-fashioned cry. By dinnertime, I felt a hundred percent better about almost everything.

The next morning, I was a little stiff in all parts of my body, but I really didn't have much time to think about it. All the girls were very excited because the boys were coming. In fact, everybody ran around shouting, "The boys are coming, the boys are coming," as if they were coming with gold or something.

Mr. Hildebrande called us around the flagpole and explained that we should think of the boys' visit as if they were our braves returning from the hunt and we were the fair maidens ready to sing them ashore. It sounded positively sickening. If Mr. Hildebrande had ever heard of women's lib, he was choosing to ignore it for the great occasion.

Mr. Hildebrande posted lookouts by the side of the lake near Daddy's tree platform. He was still up there asleep in his bag, so they had to content themselves with standing on the shoreline and scanning the waters for the first sight of the boys' canoes. The rest of us were supposed to be gathering flowers from the fields to strew in their path. I was certainly not going to run around the fields gathering flowers for anybody, especially the boys. For one thing, going into the fields meant being bitten by every insect that ever lived. Serena began to tell us tales of the terrible things the boys had done on previous yearly trips, like the time they took the roof off the girls' shower room. Then Serena called for volunteers to help prepare a special welcome she had in mind.

The rest of us lined up at a long table in the dining room to pack the box lunches our visiting braves would eat after their heroic paddle across the lake. The chef brought out huge platters of fried chicken, buckets of apples, piles of muffins, and a giant kettle of fresh-cooked corn on the cob. It was the best meal we'd ever seen coming out of the camp kitchen. A carton of flat boxes appeared, and we were first supposed to assemble the boxes and then pack them, like an assembly line. Each girl had charge of one box and took turns standing at the head of the table waiting for the contents to be passed along in a line. Mr. Hildebrande gave us detailed instructions on just how much of everything to put into each box, and then he went away to prepare a welcoming speech.

We lined up and began passing the fried chicken. As each delectable piece passed hand to hand on the way to its box, each girl took a bite of it. Who could resist? It was the first decent food many had eaten all summer. The corn on the cob followed, and each girl took a bite of that also. The apples and muffins followed, and they were really delicious. The way it worked out, every boy would be presented with his very own box containing the bare bones from a piece of chicken, a naked cob from an ear of corn, and the core of an apple sprinkled with tiny muffin crumbs. It didn't look very appetizing, but it had tasted great.

When we were done, we tied each box with a lovely little ribbon topped off with a bow and waited for our heroes from across the water. Mr. Hildebrande called us to the banks of the dear old dismal swamp and gave us a pep talk about hospitality and camp tradition. From the way he carried on about it, we all knew that somehow he was making money on the deal. Finally, when he was satisfied that we were all filled with the spirit of the occasion, he stood shakily in the middle of a canoe, and our head counselor paddled it a few feet out onto the lake for the welcoming ceremony.

We happy, welcoming maidens were supposed to

sing the camp song behind him in hushed tones and offer up our bowed boxed lunches in tribute. No one knew any of the words exactly—most of us didn't even know there was an official camp song—so we decided to sing "So Long, It's Been Good to Know You" instead. Unfortunately, no one knew the words to that one either, so we contented ourselves just singing the title several times in a row.

Our visitors appeared in several canoes, surrounding one mysterious-looking rowboat, containing a mysterious-looking cargo and three fiendishly giggling boys. Just as Mr. H. was about to begin his speech and we were about to stop singing, the canoes parted and the rowboat came closer. The mysterious-looking object turned out to be a battery-driven tennis ball launcher. Small, but deadly. The boys opened fire with their infernal machine, and it began to hurl tennis balls furiously in our direction. They bounced off our heads and rears, and the first thing we did was to drop the box lunches. It looked like the beginnings of a major rout, and they weren't even ashore yet. Naturally, we did what any sensible, serious bunch of people would do in that situation. We screamed and howled and ran in every direction.

Then suddenly our counselor and her volunteers came running out of the woods and rallied us all. Serena was waving a bicycle tire inner tube which she'd cut in half. She tied each end to a crook in a tree like a giant slingshot and began lobbing water balloons at the canoes with fearsome accuracy and force. The first balloon hit Mr. Hildebrande in the back of the head and capsized his canoe. The second and third balloons scored direct hits on the rowboat, but the boys sped up the ball thrower's engine and rained a hail of tennis balls at her contraption, driving her momentarily back.

She struggled forward and blew her whistle, and two of the older girls came running down the hill, each pushing a wheelbarrow, while we formed a line and passed the balloons. We were almost out of ammunition by the time the wheelbarrows reached us, and the tennis balls were still whizzing all around us like fuzzy missiles. This is what Francis Scott Key must have been talking about when he wrote "The Star-Spangled Banner." I personally was very glad we'd eaten their chicken and was just sorry there hadn't been more of it.

We gathered around the wheelbarrows and saw that one of them contained the camp's supply of lacrosse sticks. Serena quickly passed them out, one each. The other wheelbarrow contained our second secret weapon: a generous portion of the huge pile behind the stable where all the used straw and horse droppings were heaped until they lost their potency and odor and became valuable fertilizer. The boys had no way of knowing that the dreaded substance was no longer pungent. All they saw were nets loaded with horse chips being launched in their direction. Our aim wasn't all that good, but we made up for it in sheer quantity as more wheelbarrows arrived.

One by one the boys abandoned their canoes and jumped into the sludge rather than face their terrible fate. The whole tribe of them swam for the banks of the lake. Wil was one of the first ashore. The rowboat continued the fight until it took six direct hits and its crew of three threw themselves overboard. It was a complete victory, but we had our casualties, too. The launcher on the rowboat continued to hurl tennis balls with a mind of its own. Somehow its fire got concentrated on poor Daddy's sleeping platform, which wasn't exactly the most solidly built thing in the world in the first place. The struts that held it up took several hard blows and collapsed. This caused the deck to sag at one end and then collapse at a forty-five degree angle. The next thing anyone knew, sleeping Daddy and his sleeping bag went sliding off the edge and into the lake like a burial at sea.

Daddy opened his eyes in midair, looking very similar to a mummy coming to life. Then he and his bag plunged straight to the bottom of the lake and a moment later came rocketing back up and out of the water as if they'd been shot to the surface by a submarine. They plopped back onto the water and began to float away until the counselors from the boys' camp jumped back in and dragged them ashore.

"What happened?" was all Daddy could say as he lay there, still in his soggy bag. That's exactly what he'd asked me at the show. It occurred to me that my father didn't always pay enough attention to what was going on around him. Maybe that's why Mama and he weren't getting along.

My grandmother had come down to the shore with my mother to watch the festivities, and they stood over Daddy and just stared at him. Mama looked relieved to see him ashore, but couldn't help laughing.

"What happened?" he asked again.

"That's what I'd like to know," Grandma said, poking his drenched bag with her cane. "What were you doing spending the night in a tree?"

Grandma wanted to know why he hadn't been home all night with his wife, where she said he belonged. Daddy mumbled something about fresh air as he tried to unzip his cocoon, while Mama walked quietly backward and out of the picture. Daddy was trying to act casual about getting out of his wet sleeping bag while trying to answer questions, but finally they had to cut him free with a pocketknife. He stood up, leaking water from every pocket, and tried to tell everybody how much the bag had cost. But Grandma wouldn't let him change the subject, and he proceeded to say something about scientific research and mosquito control.

I couldn't believe my ears. There was my very own father telling a big fat lie right in front of his mother-in-law. It's shocking what parents will do sometimes. Whenever I'd tell a lie about how much homework I had, for instance, he'd always go into his honesty speech and look disappointed in me. That always made me feel bad, so I took this opportunity to go into his honesty speech and look very disappointed in him. But he was so wet and upset about his bag that he hardly even noticed.

Wil joined us a little hesitantly. I don't think he wanted his friends to know that the man in the tree was his father. I can't say I blamed him. I felt the same way about it, but in my case, the girls already knew. Wil certainly looked good, and I was glad to see him. He'd grown about four inches over the summer and had matured in other ways too, particularly about our parental situation. Later on, he told me he'd thought long and hard about it and had reconciled himself to the burden of two birthday parties a year.

It turned out to be a wonderful day full of games and excitement. We had three-legged races, which we won, and feet-in-a-sack races, which we won. Then we passed out the box lunches and had a tug-of-war into a pit of mud, which the boys won. Afterwards, everybody trooped across the road for the barbecue in which Albert outdid himself. His spareribs were the highlight of the day, and the only food the boys had gotten their hands on. Everybody got to like Daddy too, partly because his potato salad was so good, and there was plenty of it. Grandma made a big hit with us all when she gave Nurse Maxwell fifty dollars and sent her to town to buy a huge amount of ice cream.

After everyone was fed and happy, Grandma woke Old Tim and helped him get behind the wheel of the Packard for their very slow drive home. Before Grandma left, she called Mama and Daddy to the rear window of her car and told them that if she suspected what she thought she suspected, they were going to find themselves the poor parents of wealthy children, if and when she ever went over yonder, as she put it. Wil and I decided that between one thing and another, all this divorce stuff might not be so bad after all.

When it got dark, Mr. Hildebrande lit a huge bonfire down by the lake and we all sat around it and sang sad songs. It was lovely. It was almost romantic, if you like that sort of thing. Serena seemed to like it. She disappeared with one of the boys' camp counselors. Mama and Daddy seemed to like it too, and Wil and I got the shock of our lives when halfway through the night our parents walked slowly off together holding hands. Wil and I decided that maybe they were trying to do us out of our inheritance.

When it came time for the boys to leave, they lit their lanterns, bailed out their canoes, and set out over the water for the return trip to camp.

We stood on the shore holding lighted candles, watching them go. Some girls sang softly, some threw flowers, some even cried a tear or two, and Serena's counselor friend had to jump in the water and swim after the canoes to catch up.

All of us felt warm and good inside. Jen said she'd never, ever forget the night, or us, or anything. Lily's mind was finally off her chest, and even Joan was reluctant to go back to bed.

Chapter Twelve

The next morning we were allowed to sleep late, partly because the chef had quit in a snit the night before when everyone told him that Albert was a better cook than he. Nobody was going to miss his oatmeal, and I wasn't all that anxious to get up and out for cold cereal. I was enjoying my snooze and was in the middle of a dream where Blue and I had to swim across the lake in the middle of the night to find Wil and his friends, who were lost at the top of a mountain. Naturally, we did just fine. Then, after a parade of gratitude and thanks, we won the whole Olympics all by ourselves.

It was wonderful. Just as they were about to award us all three medals, Jen woke me up with the interesting news that everyone's clean underwear was gone from the cabin. She'd gotten up early because she happens to like Rice Krispies and decided to pack for her trip home. That's when she made the startling discovery.

"Gone?" I asked, wishing she'd at least waited until the bronze, silver, and gold had been safely hung around my neck. "What do you mean, *gone?*"

"Gone," she said, "as in, not here anymore."

I raised myself on my elbows and looked around the room. "You mean our underwear is gone? All of it?"

"The girl catches on quickly," Jen said, sitting on my bed.

"But," I asked, still dazed and wondering whether I could dream the rest of my dream before they gave my medals to someone else, if I went right back to sleep, "who would steal our clean underwear?"

"A hygienic pervert," Jen suggested. "How should I know who'd take it? Why didn't they at least take our dirty underwear, and wash and dry it maybe, and return it neatly folded?"

Poor Lily was almost beside herself as she searched her ransacked trunk again and again for her most precious possession, the tiger-skin brassiere that she still hadn't gotten the chance to wear. Joan woke up and we told her what had happened, but she didn't seem to care. She swung her feet out of bed and was content to drape a sheet around herself sari-style until it was time to go to sleep again or someone did the laundry. I pulled on a pair of camp shorts. It felt a little weird not having anything on underneath.

We talked it over while Lily looked under all the beds. At first we suspected Serena, but she appeared at our door a few minutes later wrapped in a towel and told us all to assemble around the flagpole for purposes of identification.

"Who do you suppose they want us to identify?" Jen wondered.

I thought Serena meant that we had to identify ourselves for some strange reason. Lily said that it seemed a little late in the season for formalities.

"If they don't know us by now," she said glumly, "what difference does it make?"

What Serena had meant, though, was that we were supposed to assemble to identify our clean underwear.

It seemed that while we were being so nice to the boys around the campfire, singing them songs and getting all misty, a group of them had been busy making off with our unprotected dainties. Then, after raiding our private belongings, they had the nerve to run them up the flagpole in the dark, where the coming of dawn found them flapping in the breeze.

We hurried to the flagpole outside the dining room. There was our underwear, waving in the breeze, high over our heads. It looked like some sort of distress signal from a wayward women's residence someplace. Our most intimate apparel out in the open, for all the world to see. I was just glad I didn't have any holes, tears, or loose elastic to worry about. Even so, as embarrassing as it was for us all, it was worst for Lily.

Everyone was looking up, and there, right at the tip-top of the pole, flying proudly in the place of honor, was her treasured tiger-skin bra, straight from Sweden and waving hello. It seemed to attract everyone's attention and caused a lot of snide comments and even more speculation as to just who belonged to and in it. At first everybody looked at Serena, but she just looked back and said she wouldn't be caught dead in such a creation. I thought that was unkind and, besides, I really don't think she meant it. I told Lily that Serena was just jealous, and she and Jen agreed with me, so we knew we were right.

Then Nurse Maxwell hurried over, and almost all

the girls turned around to stare at her. Since her friendship with Albert had started, we'd looked at her with lots of new curiosity. Nurse Maxwell just stood there and blushed, and that immediately set everyone's mind wondering. Whispers and giggles followed, and Nurse Maxwell said, "No, no. It's not mine."

Mr. Hildebrande heard the commotion and he came running to the pole, looked up, and then he blushed, too. Jen said that we should start a rumor that it belonged to him. She said it would take the heat off Lily, just in case they ran out of suspects and turned on us. Mr. Hildebrande rubbed his eyes and then he just stood there staring up, too. It took a few minutes for his amazement to wear off enough for him to ask Nurse Maxwell to take charge and lower the colors. Before he left, he took one more look at our topmost pennant and then hurried off, leaving Nurse Maxwell to do her duty.

She went to the base of the pole and had a lot of trouble undoing the knot the culprits had left us. Obviously, one of them had been a Boy Scout before turning to a life of crime. She finally got the rope untied by using her teeth. Then she began to lower the line of undies very slowly. She disconnected each piece and held it out at arm's length as one by one we raised our hands and came forward to claim what was ours. You can certainly tell a lot about people by what they choose to wear under their clothes. Serena, for instance, seemed very partial to scarlet flower motifs with lots of lace. No one was really surprised when she identified the shocking frillies as her own. Slowly, most of the belongings were returned to their rightful owners, but none of the girls seemed ready to leave until everything had been accounted for. They all stood around clutching their property, just waiting for the big event of the day.

Since Lily's treasure had been the first up, it naturally became the last down. Lily, Jen, and I kind of shuffled around hoping everyone else would just go away. But every girl in camp was still shuffling around with us, waiting breathlessly to see who had the nerve to claim it. I really had to give Lily a great deal of credit and respect, because when Nurse Maxwell finally loosened the bra from the line and dangled it in our faces by one strap, Lily took a deep breath and then marched right up and called it hers. Then she marched right back, only this time she had to march through numerous people holding their sides and rolling around the ground in glee. Sometimes my faith in the basic goodness of the human race gets severely shaken. That's one of the reasons I often prefer the company of horses.

Serena came through for us, though. She walked to our side and at the top of her lungs more or less told everybody there to can it. Then she put a comforting arm around Lily's shoulder and marched with us back to our bunks. She may have been weird, but you could depend on her in a pinch. What more could you want in a counselor? She helped to restore my trust in my fellow creatures that day—well, some of them, anyway.

We finished our packing, and all the girls in our cabin took an oath right then and there to hate boys forever until we were old enough to like them.

We exchanged addresses and telephone numbers, and hugs and promises, and soon it was time to leave. With all the excitement going on, it hadn't occurred to me to wonder just where Daddy had spent the night. I didn't think he'd been up on the collapsed platform clinging to its side, and his sleeping bag was still just a wet heap of down by the shore. I didn't think about it at all until Nurse Maxwell stopped by to say good-bye and giggled the information that my father had stayed in the same house with my mother. That may not sound shocking to you, but it certainly took me by surprise. I also never dreamed that my parents' sleeping habits would ever be the subject of an entire camp's conversation.

My luggage was all packed by the time Mama and Daddy came to get me in our car. That was another shock. To say that they acted as if they were a couple of kids disgustingly in love is to put it mildly by anybody's standards. Daddy was behind the wheel and Mama in the passenger seat when the car came to a stop in front of my cabin. Daddy leapt out, ran around the car, and opened the door for my mother. She smiled at him sweetly, and he held out his hand to help her out, for God's sake, and she smiled at him again. It's amazing how far some people will go just not to be disinherited. Maybe they'd been sitting too close to the bonfire the night before and had gotten overheated or something. Whatever the reason, their little romantic glow had certainly been rekindled. I wasn't sure I was quite ready for all this affection at my doorstep. At least not from my parents.

I looked around for Albert, but he was no longer following their car in his car for Mama's safety. In fact, he was nowhere in sight at all. Mama told me that since the house and cottage were rented through Labor Day, and available eternally, there was lots of talk about Albert staying on awhile with Nurse Maxwell. There was even talk about his staying on permanently! Mama and Daddy made them a present of our dog. They congratulated themselves on how unselfish it was of them to let Fluff live in the great outdoors with Albert instead of our cramped city apartment. They had both agreed that it was much better for all concerned, Daddy in particular. Did this mean that Daddy was coming home with us to reclaim his comfy chair?

Daddy explained psychologically that it seemed Albert had lost his heart to Nurse Maxwell and was considering giving up his law practice for the peace of the country and the joy of weaving sandals for a living. As it turned out, everybody's friend Mr. Hildebrande owned a thriving handcrafts store and claimed he could sell all that Albert gave him. Albert had said that he'd never felt so much at peace as when he was working with his hands. It sounded to me like he'd lost his mind as well. It must have been all that fresh country air. City people just aren't used to it. The whole world was going crazy right before my eyes.

Mama came into my cabin to help me with my things and hugged me, then Daddy came into my cabin and hugged me, too. You'd think I was leaving instead of just coming back. I was in something of a state of shock, so I let them load my bags into the trunk while I went down to the stable and hugged Blue. I promised him I'd come back next summer, and he looked at me as if he understood. He always looked at me as if he understood. That was one of the things I liked most about him. I think he understood how important that was to me.

Jen and Lily were at the stable saying good-bye to their horses too, and after we all promised each other to come back next year and room together, we went back to the cabin feeling just a little weepy. Their parents still hadn't shown up by the time mine were ready to go, and they waved and shouted good-bye as we drove off to get Wil. I left them with a note for Joan, because she'd gone back to sleep. We drove out the front gate past the rented house, and there was Albert sitting cross-legged on the lawn, chewing leather or something. I think perhaps he was trying to soften it, but I fully expected that the next time I saw him, he'd be wearing a straitjacket. Mama said he'd come to his senses along with the first snowfall.

Fluff saw us driving by and chased us down the road, barking at the tires. Daddy said he hoped it never snowed, because he wanted Fluff to have a decent life in the country with Albert.

Mama waved to Albert and said it was obviously a mid-life crisis he was going through and would probably snap out of it as soon as Nurse Maxwell took off her makeup. Daddy said that even if that did happen, they would let Albert keep Fluff forever, because they were so good for each other. Mama agreed. Everybody was being so nice and unselfish that I started to get a headache. Then they both sighed, and we went up and down and around the mountain to my brother's camp.

Wil was sitting on his duffel bag, waiting for us outside his tent, when we arrived. His living conditions were even more primitive than mine had been. At least my accommodations had wood walls and a roof, such as it was. He didn't even have windows. No wonder the boys were so mean.

We came to a stop and Daddy leapt out of the car again like a spring, and I wondered what had happened to the arthritis he always claimed he was getting when it was time to put the garbage in the hall. He once again held the door open for Mama and gave her his hand to help her out. Then Mama smiled and hugged Wil, and Daddy smiled and hugged Wil, and Wil looked at me in wonder. I just shrugged. I wasn't sure what he was wondering about, but if he was wondering whether I was going to hug him, there was no chance. Not after what he and his hoodlum friends had done to our underwear.

Wil got into the car and asked me what was going on? I told him I wasn't certain, but it seemed to me that reconciliation was in the air. Wil said he felt like feeling carsick already. It wasn't as if we didn't want them to be together or anything. What we still wanted was a little consistency on their parts. We'd barely gotten ourselves used to being the products of a broken home, and here it was looking mended again. If things kept up as they were, our parents would be ganging up on us again in no time. Both of us began to think of piña coladas and Shirley Temples as a fond memory.

We settled down quietly in the back seat for the ride home and waited for the arguments we knew and loved to begin. Instead, everything up front was positively ducky. Mama promised Daddy not to be so extravagant in the future, and Daddy promised Mama not to be so cheap. Then Daddy promised Mama not to be resentful because she made more money than he did last year, and Mama promised Daddy not to rub it in. Mama promised to take her fair turns parking the car, and Daddy promised not to buy her any more appliances as gifts.

She really liked that. She said she was happy he understood that sometimes she liked personal presents on special occasions and not household furnishings or things to eat, no matter how nice they were, she added nicely, and said she hoped that didn't sound selfish. He said he was glad she'd brought it to his attention and said she didn't have a selfish bone in her body. She renounced bickering, and he renounced bickering.

We were being driven home by two complete strangers.

Mama moved as close to Daddy as her seat belt would allow, and they started to talk about how long they'd been married, and how fast time flew, and how their anniversary was right around the corner. They continued to talk about how long they'd been married, and how fast time flew, and how their anniversary was right around the corner.

They started to talk about the pleasures of family life and having kids, and Daddy looked at Wil and me through the rearview mirror and smiled lovingly. And Mama turned around as much as she could and looked at Wil and me and smiled lovingly, too. Then they looked at each other all cozy and self-satisfied, and I almost expected them to announce that they'd decided to have another child.

All this love was starting to get on my nerves. I'd grown quite accustomed to a stony silence while traveling, but they didn't seem inclined to stop talking about how lucky they were, and I began to feel positively faint. It seemed to me if they were all that lucky they shouldn't be wasting their time talking about it. They should be playing the lottery or something.

I wondered if I was lucky, and the car's engine started to overheat and it momentarily took their minds off all their happiness, so I decided that maybe I was. It was about time, too. A few more gushes from their direction and I was the one who was going to get carsick.

Steam started to billow out of the car's radiator, so Daddy turned on the windshield wipers. Then Mama smiled and asked him if he didn't think it was a good idea to pull into the next gas station, and he said, "Whatever you think best," and smiled at her smile, and Wil put a finger down his throat and began to gag. We drove into the next service area, and while Daddy waited for the engine to cool so he could add water, Wil, Mama, and I went into the restaurant. Wil ordered french fries, I my Coke, and then we waited for Mama to ask for her coffee and a blueberry muffin. We needed to know that something in our world was still all right. Instead, she ordered a cup of coffee and a Danish pastry. At first we thought she had a new client, but she didn't even check the pastry to see if it had enough cheese. She just ate it. Then she ordered a container of coffee to go! And when she paid the check, she didn't write it all down in her little expenses book. My own mother was losing her marbles!

We went back to the car and discovered that Daddy had already bought a container of coffee from a machine near the gas pumps. He still had half left. Then he did an amazing thing, for my father anyway—he threw his unfinished container away and said he'd rather drink hers. My own father, acting as if coffee grew on trees. They smiled again at each other like two victims of lockjaw.

When we got back on the highway, Mama looked over at the gas gauge and asked Daddy if he'd filled the tank. He said he hadn't but would stop at the next station—which he drove right by. I think wasting the coffee money was on his mind. I imagined that I saw Mama stiffen just a little bit. Not much though. Certainly nothing even halfway like the stiffening I'd seen her do in the past. Then the engine started to boil a little and Mama said that maybe it was time they thought about getting a new car, and I noticed that the hairs on the back of Daddy's neck suddenly stood out just a touch. Wil noticed it too, and we looked at each other and waited for the instant explosion, but none came.

They didn't talk much after that, and finally Daddy stopped for gas. Wil and I had our usual, and Mama just had a ginger ale, but this time she didn't buy Daddy a container of coffee, and this time he hadn't bought one either. She said she thought that he had, and he said he thought that she had. But they smiled at each other anyway, and it seemed to me that they'd make a good advertisement for successful cosmetic dentistry.

We rode on in silence and had to stop a few more times to feed the engine water. It was dark when we finally reached the city, and there were no parking spaces on our whole block. Daddy double-parked in front of the house, and our doorman welcomed Wil and Mama and me home. He ignored Daddy, because he hadn't heard the good news. Then, when he noticed that one of the bags we'd unloaded onto the sidewalk belonged to Daddy, he said hello as if he'd never been away.

We all helped with the luggage, and Mama suggested that Daddy put the car in a garage.

"I thought you weren't going to be so extravagant," he chuckled.

"I thought you weren't going to be so cheap," she chuckled back.

Then Daddy said that he'd given it a lot of thought and had figured out that it was Mama's turn to park the car. She said that he had figured wrong and he should give it a lot more thought. We were almost one big happy family again.

Daddy circled the block until he found a space, and

then he came up to the apartment without being announced by the doorman. Mama didn't jog into the kitchen when he walked in, and Daddy sat in his chair without brushing it off first. Things were back to normal in our house.

In the weeks that followed, Wil and I tried to cultivate a taste for plain ginger ale. Not that we had much of an opportunity for even that. Most times when the subject of eating out came up, Daddy would say we'd eaten out enough for two families already. Then he'd say that there was nothing like a home-made hamburger and freshly frozen mixed vegetables. I thought I was back at Chucalucup.

In October, we celebrated their anniversary. Wil and I got Mama a small enamel pin in the shape of a turtle that looked absolutely real, and Daddy a pencil-shaped gauge to measure the amount of air in his tires. They both loved their presents. Then my mother gave my father a very nice cardigan sweater he said he'd wear while he was talking to his patients. Then Daddy gave Mama a beautiful toaster.

Mama laughed lightly when she pulled it out of its box. Daddy looked delighted. For a few minutes we sat around the living room looking at the toaster. "I knew you'd like it. It does six slices at once," he said, in case Mama thought two of the slots were for drying her nails. Then he got up from where he'd been closely inspecting the very complicated controls. "I know what. I'll go buy some English muffins."

Mama said as long as he was going, he should get some raspberry jam as well, and then she got up and went to the phone. Wil looked at me and asked if this meant we could make plans for a cruise again this year. I said I thought we should start planning for camp. I knew definitely that Mama had wanted perfume.

Daddy followed Mama to the phone and asked her if she really liked the toaster. She said that it was the nicest toaster that she'd ever seen. She said that if there was one thing she knew about him, it was that he could be counted on to buy a first-rate appliance.

Daddy was very pleased. Mama said she'd learned to accept that as one of his gift-buying idiosyncrasies. Then she added that life, and married life in particular, sometimes involved putting up with others' idiosyncrasies, and Daddy quickly agreed. Then he asked whether she thought he should have gotten the eight-slice model.

Mama didn't answer. She just smiled warmly at him while she waited for her call to go through. Then she told Albert to please send back Fluff.